The Brokenhearted Christian

BOOK ONE

JOHN HUFFT

ISBN 978-1-63575-956-3 (Paperback)
ISBN 978-1-64028-316-9 (Hard Cover)
ISBN 978-1-63575-957-0 (Digital)

Christian Faith Publishing, Inc.
296 Chestnut Street
Meadville, PA 16335
www.christianfaithpublishing.com

Printed in the United States of America

"For I know the plans I have for you," declares the Lord, "plans to prosper you and not to harm you, plans to give you hope and a future."

Jeremiah 29:11

CHAPTER ONE

A New Beginning

The colony of seagulls walked the white sandy beach scavenging for any kind of nourishment. Some dug in trash, while others flew over the Pacific, soaring high, searching for their morning breakfast. It was a relaxing pleasure to sit on the beach and watch the gulls rummage for food. To experience the smell of the ocean and hear the sound of the waves crashing was a time to take in and exhale a deep breath of peace. The beach was a perfect spot where one could feel the cool wind on his face while digging his feet into the velvety white sand that felt like soft baby powder as it squished between his toes.

"I know what I'm going to wish for this time," said the brown-haired little girl as she closed her eyes before she threw a pebble across the water. It skipped just two times; she hoped for more.

"What did ya wish for?" asked Joshua.

"Well, I can't tell you, or else it won't come true, silly."

Joshua looked out toward the ocean, waited for the water to calm, picked up a pebble out of his bag, made his wish, then chucked the stone across the water, skipping it several times.

"Lucky!"

"Not bad, eh?"

The little girl was a bit jealous. She hadn't mastered a three skip yet.

"It's okay, you don't have to tell me what you wished for either. I want it to be special and come true for you too." The little girl inched closer to Joshua. Joshua closed his bag of pebbles and wrapped his arm around her as they both sat on the warm sand admiring the ocean's beauty.

"You promise you'll never leave me?" asked the little girl.

"Of course, I promise, Gingersnap," smiled Joshua.

The little girl looked up into Joshua's eyes with a forlorn expression on her face, "Then, where am I?"

Joshua's smile ceased. The little girl disappeared in an instant. "Amari!" Joshua screamed, and immediately woke up with sweat dripping from his brow.

It was bad enough that Daniel Carpenter had to move his family for his real estate business to Missouri the summer before Joshua's senior year, but to make matters worse, destructive weather patterns across the states created several problems for the Carpenter family's move.

The heavy storms caused long delays in traffic and seemed to follow them from one town to the next. After a fifteen-hour exhausting drive, they pulled into a Holiday Inn Express in Salt Lake City, Utah. When they arrived at their long-awaited oasis for the night, they found the hotel beds were a welcome refuge from the horrendous nature outdoors. As the rain continued to downpour outside, the Carpenter family, tired and worn out, each drifted into their own tranquil world.

The next morning, the rain was still pouring down. Not only had it rained all night, but it hailed so hard, it caused damage to the rental moving truck.

"Are we responsible for the damages?" Mrs. Carpenter asked as she viewed the damaged vehicle from the hotel room window.

"Now, honey, I wouldn't think we would be responsible for something Mother Nature caused," Mr. Carpenter responded. Mr. Carpenter wasn't a tall man. He was average height with arms of steel according to Mrs. Carpenter. While Mrs. Carpenter admired her husband's arms, Mr. Carpenter adored his wife's short reddish blond hair along with her captivating smile.

Mrs. Carpenter sighed deeply. She was ready for this trip to be over. She also couldn't wait to get into her new home and start decorating. She loved to rearrange their home over and over to keep busy. With the packing of boxes over the past few months, and not being able to room design, Mrs. Carpenter couldn't wait to make their new house their next home. She sat at the edge of the bed for a minute in a cogitative silence, trying to set her worries aside, but the lightning outside brought her to her feet.

"Hey, honey, they have a continental breakfast!" said Mr. Carpenter excitedly.

Mr. Carpenter loved continental breakfasts served in hotels. He particularly loved the ones with a hot breakfast bar.

"Amen to that!" Joshua approved as he stretched out of bed. Mr. and Mrs. Carpenter looked at each other with a blank stare as they raised their eyebrows.

"You both better get ready, or there's not going to be any breakfast," said Mrs. Carpenter.

After throwing on some clothes, they walked into the breakfast area and saw an assortment of delicious food items before them. Hotcakes, biscuits and gravy, and sausage and bacon were just a few of the items available. After the long night, they were hungry and ready to eat. Mr. Carpenter had blessed the food before they dove into their hot breakfast. While eating, they discussed the best route to take for their drive ahead. After about thirty minutes of weighing their options, they finished eating and checked out of the hotel. Although they enjoyed a great night's sleep and a fabulous breakfast, trying to have a relaxing drive was not happening as the weather outside was once again refusing to cooperate.

"This rain is not going to let up, and I sure hope…" Boom! Mr. Carpenter hit a pothole on the road as he choked on his words, grabbing the steering wheel tight. He pulled to the side of the road as the tire went flat.

"Great! Just great! Of all the things we need right now, a flat tire just tops them all," Mr. Carpenter burst out.

"It's okay, Dad. I'll help you change it." Joshua hopped out of the car to get the jack ready.

"Thank you, son," Mr. Carpenter said as he sighed deeply.

They both headed out to change the tire while Mrs. Carpenter prayed to herself. Soaking wet, and twenty minutes later, the Carpenters were back on the road again. Although the storm continued throughout their entire trip, they finally reach their destination—their new home.

The drive from Rockaway Beach, Oregon, to Red Gleans, Missouri, was over. Although they were delighted to finally be home, everyone was so worn-out, they decided to unpack the moving truck in the morning. They grabbed some blankets and pillows from their truck, spread them out on the living room floor, and called it a night. It has been a rough ride. They were all burned out. Even though it was a tiring trip, the Carpenter family was looking forward to a new adventure in their life. But not just any adventure, they were looking for a change—a change of scenery, a chance to meet new people, and experience a whole new life.

The next morning turned out to be beautiful. It was a perfect day to unpack one's past into the present. The sun shined through the living room window, brightening up the place. The house was a four-bed-room, two-bath dwelling with a three-car garage and an upstairs loft area. It was home.

"Time to get up and at 'em," yawned Mr. Carpenter.

Mrs. Carpenter and Joshua were reluctant to get up.

"I know we are all worn out from our trip, but we have a lot to do today. First things first, we need to make some coffee," said Mr. Carpenter.

"I have bad news," replied Mrs. Carpenter. "The coffee container spilled when we hit the pothole. I didn't want to say anything at the time because of the situation."

"Well, I'll take Joshua into town, and we can stop by the store and pick up some," Mr. Carpenter said.

Joshua finally dragged himself off the carpeted living room floor and got dressed. He and his father unhitched their car from the moving truck and headed into town.

Now that they were in a new city, it clicked with Joshua, and he felt overwhelmed on the upcoming changes he had to deal with.

"Why on earth did we have to move here? Why did you decide to go up and move me on my senior year?" Joshua asked in an annoyed manner.

"We have been through this, Joshua," responded Mr. Carpenter as he pulled up to a stoplight.

"I know, we have talked about it. I guess it's just now hitting me since we are here now," Joshua replied.

"Everything is going to work out. I promise," Mr. Carpenter said.

The two headed to a local coffee shop to pick up three cups of joe.

"I've got to find a restroom in this place. Go ahead and order us three large coffees and see if they have any donuts," Mr. Carpenter gave money to Joshua, then headed to the men's room around the corner.

"I recommend the strawberry frosted with sprinkles," a girl behind the counter said.

"Yeah, I was thinking the same..."Joshua lifted his head up after glancing at the plethora of donuts he found in a glass case and forgot what he was going to say.

The girl laughed. "Are you ok?"

Joshua shook his head. "Uh, yeah. Sorry. Um... I... uh... yes... will take a dozen of your donuts strawberry sprinkled with frosted."

The girl laughed again. "You want a dozen of what?" she asked.

"Sorry. Uh, I have no idea what I was saying." Joshua was embarrassed.

"I think I know what you want," said the girl.

"You do?" asked Joshua.

"You want three large coffees and a dozen of the strawberry-frosted sprinkled donuts," said the girl with confidence.

"Wow, you're good," said Joshua.

"Yeah, well, I overheard you talking with..."

"Oh, that was my dad."

"Gotcha! I overheard you talking with *your dad* that you wanted coffee and donuts."

"Yes, that is correct. Thank you," said Joshua.

"You're welcome. Give me just a minute." The blond-haired girl worked toward getting Joshua's order ready.

"So, how are you able to be out of school today?" Joshua questioned the girl.

She finished boxing up the donuts and handed them to Joshua.

"I have to ask," she chuckled. "You're not from around here, are you?"

"It's obvious, isn't it?"

She smiled and leaned down toward him, looked him in the eyes and whispered, "Yes! It's very obvious."

A grin formed on Joshua's face.

"And just an FYI, it's Saturday. And another FYI, school doesn't start until next week," said the girl.

Joshua lifted up his index finger and pointed it in the air.

"Right. Right you are," he said.

The girl smiled back at Joshua.

"Oh, you want to know my name?" said the girl as she placed her hand on her chest referring to herself.

Joshua looked down and read the name tag for the first time. "Mary," Joshua said.

"That is me!" said Mary.

"Let me start over. My name is Joshua. It is very nice to meet you." Joshua reached out his hand toward her.

"My name is Mary, and it is very nice to meet you as well, Joshua." She shook his hand and could not seem to let go.

Joshua and Mary continued shaking hands, smiling and staring at each other.

"You okay, son?" asked Mr. Carpenter.

Joshua came out of his trance.

"Hey, Dad! Hi! Uh, this is Mary."

"Well, hello there, Mary. Pleased to meet you." Mr. Carpenter shook Mary's hand.

"It's 'pleased to meet you' as well, Joshua's dad," said Mary with a grin.

"Come on son, we best be going. I'll let you say your goodbyes." Mr. Carpenter walked out the coffee shop.

"Well, I must be going, and I hope to see you around soon." Joshua hoped for a "yes."

"Yes. I would like that very much," said Mary.

"Great! Okay, well, bye." Joshua ran into the door.

Mary laughed and smiled.

"Goodbye," she said.

Joshua took one more look, waved, and smiled, then walked out the door.

"You know, Dad, I think we are going to be okay here," Joshua said as he shook his head up and down.

"You know, son, I believe that you're right."

As the weekend went on, the Carpenters continued to unpack their belongings into their new home. Mrs. Carpenter was elated with all the decorating ahead of her. Mr. Carpenter was getting ready, planning for his new job. Joshua was already unpacked, and although school was starting in just a few days, he had just one person on his mind, Mary.

CHAPTER TWO

High School

It was the first day of school for the students of James River High. The year was 2008. It was your typical first day of school. School buses covered the streets. Children carried their backpacks with pens, pencils, notebooks, folders, and all the necessary supplies needed for their first day. Classrooms filled with school desks, study course books, and of course, teachers—and not just any teachers, high school teachers. They were ready to open a world of knowledge for all the students. One teacher in particular, Mr. Lindwell, the creative writing teacher, strived to help his students succeed in a way that would have an impact on their lives forever. His goal was to help his students reach deep within themselves and write what genuinely inspired them. Joshua was fortunate to be placed in Mr.

Lindwell's class. Mr. Lindwell was so popular; his classroom was generally packed. His students loved him. They called him, "Mr. Dwell."

Joshua, although new to the school, had no problems making friends. His first encounter was with a student named Benjamin Underwood. Benjamin was a scruffy individual. His hair rarely combed. Jeans and T-shirt were his style. Benjamin noticed Joshua with a puzzled look on his face as he reviewed his class schedule.

"You new here, bub?" Benjamin asked Joshua.

"Yeah, I'm trying to find my first period. Creative writing."

"Oh, yeah? You write?" asked Benjamin.

"I'm good with words," said Joshua.

"Coolbeansy," responded Benjamin. Benjamin also had a way with his words.

"Well, if you walk down this hall and make a right, it should take you to room 104, creative writing. Mr. Dwell is the teacher."

"Hey, thanks! Name's Joshua."

"Benjamin."

"Nice to meet you, man. Hey, do you know of anyone hiring around town?" asked Joshua.

"I'm working over at a coffee shop on Baker Street, and we are actually looking for some help. You know how to make coffee?" asked Benjamin.

"I think I can barista it up," replied Joshua.

"Rightono, dude. Come by after school and fill out an app. I'll hook you up," said Benjamin.

"Sounds great, man. Thanks! See you then!" said Joshua.

Joshua made many friends on his first day of school. Benjamin was even in a few of his classes. Joshua was enjoying his newfound friendships and thought to himself how the move to this small city was not so bad after all. Things were looking up for him. Although he was having a fantastic day, he was curious if the blond-haired, blue-eyed, beautiful girl with the unbelievable smile he met at the coffee shop went to this school.

It was three o'clock in the afternoon. The first day of school was ending for students at James River High. At the end of each school day, there was a thirty-minute study hall class for some students. Joshua was one of those students. The one good thing about this class—no teacher. As Joshua walked around, he noticed a familiar face. It was Mary. Mary saw Joshua heading her way so she quickly turned around to avoid eye contact, as if she was looking for a particular book. She smiled to herself as Joshua moved in closer to her position.

"Any good books over here?" Joshua asked.

Mary was speechless. She took a moment, turned around, and smiled.

"Actually, there are some excellent books over here. I think this one is my favorite."

Mary held up the book, *Anne of Green Gables*.

"It's about an orphan girl who mistakenly ends up with a brother and sister who is actually attempting to adopt a boy as farm help," said Mary.

"Sounds fascinating," chuckled Joshua.

Mary was concerned with Joshua's laugh.

"Are you being sarcastic?"

"No, no. Not at all. I really think it's interesting, just not a book-reader person," said Joshua.

"Yet you are in a library for study hall?" Mary turned and walked away, hoping Joshua would follow.

"Well, I actually found out you were going to be in here, so I switched my PE class for study hall." Joshua laughed as he caught up with her.

"I kind of came out ahead. It was either sit-ups or study hall with a beautiful woman, such as yourself," Joshua said with a grin.

Mary was shocked but impressed with the compliment.

"Wow, you switched classes to be in study hall because I was in here? How did you know I was in here?"

"Well, when I was in the counselor's office this morning, I saw the name 'Mary' in this class. So I asked the guy if I could change because PE just wasn't for me. Yours truly took a chance, and it looks like I made the right decision," Joshua replied.

Mary and Joshua both smiled as they stared into each other's eyes. Joshua—with his ruffled brown hair, green eyes, and five o'clock shadow—intrigued Mary.

"So, how do you like our town? Our school?" asked Mary as she walked off again.

"To be honest, I was not looking forward to it until I met you at the coffee shop," said Joshua.

Mary smiled again and blushed. "That's really sweet of you to say! I am glad we met there too," said Mary.

"Which reminds me, I have to work tonight," said Mary.

"I'm applying at some coffee shop this afternoon. I met a guy this morning who told me to come by, but I'm not sure which one it is, though."

"What's the guy's name?" asked Mary.

Joshua thought for a minute. "Benjamin, I believe."

"Benjamin? Benjamin Underwood?" asked Mary.

"He talked really funny. He didn't give me his last name, but he said to come by after school to apply," said Joshua.

Mary laughed out loud.

"Shhh!" said one of the students.

"What's so funny?" laughed Joshua.

"Benjamin is my twin brother! The coffee shop is where I work too," Mary whispered.

"Wait, you both work at the same coffee shop? The same one I met you in? Well, how about that?"

"That's the one."

"This must be fate," said Joshua.

"Hmm, and how's that?" asked Mary.

"Well, we first met at the coffee shop. One of the first guys I ran into this morning is your brother. He told me to apply at the same coffee shop I met you in where you work. I changed classes to be with a 'Mary,' which also happened to be you. You know what that means don't you?" asked Joshua.

"And what would that be?" Mary walked away for the third time, smiling to herself.

Joshua rushed up behind her.

"I think we should go on a date. Maybe I can take you to homecoming this Friday," said Joshua.

"Oh, you do? Do you?"

The clock was winding down, and the end-of-school bell was about to ring.

"I'm not sure just yet," said Mary.

"Let me think about it, and I'll get back to you. Give me your number." Mary held out her hand.

Joshua sighed and smiled as he gave Mary his number. The classroom bell rang.

"I'll see you tonight," said Joshua.

"Well, I haven't agreed to a date just yet," said Mary.

"So, you are thinking about it, hmm?" asked Joshua.

Mary couldn't keep from smiling.

"I meant, I'll see you tonight when I come in to apply," said Joshua.

"Oh, yes. That's right. I'm assuming you know how to get to the coffee shop again?"

"Of course. It's on Baker Street," said Joshua.

"Very good! 481 Baker Street, Charlie's Coffee Shop, in case you missed the name last time," Mary said as she started to walk out the library.

"You be thinking about that date," Joshua shouted.

Mary turned, holding her books to her chest, smiled, and left the room.

"Wow. Just wow," said Joshua.

It was the end of the first day of school. Joshua, on his Diamondback Mountain Bike, headed to Charlie's Coffee Shop to put in his application. Joshua's father, Mr. Carpenter, had told him that once he found a job and was committed, he would help him get a vehicle. Joshua rolled into the parking lot, parked his bike, and entered the coffee shop. He spotted Benjamin was already there. Mary was nowhere to be found.

"Dudeski!" said Benjamin excitedly. "Good to see you again. I already talked with Charlie about you coming by."

"Awesome!" said Joshua.

"Come on over and I'll introduce you to Charlie."

Joshua and Benjamin headed to Charlie's office.

"Hey, Charlie-man, this is Joshua. I told you he was stopping by to check about the barista position." Benjamin left Joshua with Charlie.

"Well, come on in here. Thank you, Benjamin." Charlie motioned for Joshua to enter.

"So you want to be a barista, do you?" asked Charlie. Charlie was a heavier set older gentleman who slicked his gray hair back to keep it in place. He was kind-hearted and a great listener when it came to employee's problems.

"Yes, sir," Joshua replied.

Joshua and Charlie discussed the position, and as they continued, Charlie became very impressed with Joshua's attitude.

"Can you start tomorrow?" asked Charlie.

"I sure can," said Joshua.

Joshua and Charlie shook hands.

He told Benjamin about being hired, and that he was starting tomorrow. Benjamin was excited about the news and began talking with Joshua about the job. Joshua was trying to listen to Benjamin as he looked around for Mary.

"Hey, so I met your sister, Mary, today. Is she coming in tonight?"

"How do you know Mary?"

"It's kind of a long story," smiled Joshua.

"You like her!" exclaimed Benjamin.

Joshua agreed and nodded. "Yeah. Yeah, I do."

"Sweet-lee-o. She should be here any minute."

The coffee shop door opened and in walked Mary.

"*And,* there she is," Benjamin said as he pointed to Mary. Joshua turned around to see Mary walking toward him.

"Hey there, handsome," Mary said as she walked past Joshua.

"What did I just say?" Mary said to herself.

Joshua's mouth dropped, grinning from ear to ear. Joshua followed her to the back storage room.

"Well, hello yourself, beautiful," Joshua whispered to Mary as she opened the storage room door.

"I am so sorry. I'm not entirely sure what I was saying," Mary said as she turned around.

"That's okay. I'll forgive you just this once," said Joshua.

"You can't be back here," said Mary.

"Actually, I can. I was just hired by Charlie. I start tomorrow."

"Wow! That was fast. He must really like you."

"I think so too. Charlie's a great guy. Is your shift starting soon?" asked Joshua.

"Yes, I should be clocking in now."

Joshua stared and smiled at Mary as she clocked in.

"I'm very happy you got the job."

"You are?" Joshua asked excitedly.

"Of course!"

Joshua, captivated by Mary's response, gave a big smile.

"Well, I… I won't keep you unless you want me to," Joshua teased Mary.

Mary looked at Joshua and in her mind, thought that would be just fine. She smiled, turned around, and went to work.

Joshua said goodbye to Benjamin and told Mary he would call her that evening. It was a day for new friendships. It was one of the best days in Joshua's life—Marys' too.

Joshua biked home to find that his mother had decorated their entire home, getting it ready for the autumn season. Joshua walked in and plopped down on the couch in awe.

"You must like my decorating," said Mrs. Carpenter.

"Yeah," Joshua said all glassy-eyed.

"Well, that is awfully sweet of you." Mrs. Carpenter cleaned off the mantle.

"Yeah," said Joshua.

"How was school today?" Mrs. Carpenter carefully placed a vase on the mantle.

"It was great. One of the best days of my life," Joshua said in a trance-like state.

"Are you feeling okay?"

"Just fine, Mom."

Joshua headed to his room until dinner was ready. Mrs. Carpenter prepared a treat for Joshua for his first day of school—his favorite dishes—pork chops, mac and cheese, and corn with buttered rolls.

About an hour later, the dinner smell drove the Carpenter family to the kitchen table.

"Daniel, would you say grace please?" asked Mrs. Carpenter.

Mr. Carpenter blessed the meal.

"Well, son, how did today go at school?" asked Mr. Carpenter.

Joshua finally came to his senses.

"You know, Dad, I had an awesome day. There was this girl, and I can't explain it, but she was the most beautiful creature ever. I got a job and just had a really great day!"

"Wow! Well, that is great news!"

"Okay, tell me about it. What kind of job? When do you start? Wait. What? Who is this girl?" asked Mr. Carpenter surprised.

Joshua told his parents about his job and about Mary, and how she was the girl he met at the coffee shop. They had an active discussion over their family dinner.

Meanwhile, over at the Underwood's house, Mary came home from work to tell her parents about her day.

"That boy I met at the coffee shop, I saw him at school today and at work," Mary smiled as she told her parents.

Mr. & Mrs. Underwood listened as their daughter told them about her day. Mary was the happiest she had been in a long time.

Later that evening, Joshua was ready to call Mary.

"Surely she was off from work by now," he thought to himself.

It was half past nine. Joshua went through his pants pockets and fumbled through his book bags looking for Mary's number.

"Where is it?" Joshua frantically searched for the number.

He thought for a moment when his mind quickly changed gears.

"Wait a minute!" He remembered he gave Mary *his* number, and he never got *her* number.

"Ugh! What was I thinking?"

Joshua sat on his bed for a while, thinking to himself what he should do. Just as he was about to pull the hairs out of his head, his phone rang once, then stopped. He lifted up his phone from his nightstand and noticed his cell phone battery had died, causing his phone to shut off.

"No!" Joshua shouted.

He quickly plugged his phone in. "Come on! Come on!" Joshua exclaimed.

As he anticipated his phone to start up, he was getting very uncomfortable. It seemed as if everything was annoying him. His clothes felt like they were positioned awkwardly on his body. His shoes were bothering him. And to top it off, he started to itch.

"Finally!" he said.

Joshua's phone lit up as if it was a hallelujah moment. He checked the missed calls. He immediately called the number.

"Hello?" Mary answered.

"Hey, Mary, this is Joshua."

"Well, hey there!" Mary replied in an ecstatic tone.

"I'm sorry, but my phone died as you called me," said Joshua.

"Maybe it was fate that I didn't talk to you just then."

There was a pause on the other end.

"I'm kidding!" said Mary. "I'm glad you called back."

"I was going to call you but realized I didn't have your phone number. I was hoping you'd call tonight."

Mary loved the attention and comforting words.

The two talked for a while about school, about life and each other. It was time for the one question Joshua had wanted to ask.

"So," Joshua took a deep breath.

"I would really like to take you to homecoming. Would you go with me?"

Mary was wondering when he was going to ask.

"I would love... for you to take me."

"Really?" Joshua said excitedly as he quietly said yes to himself.

"But, I do have one question," said Mary.

"Okay. Ask anything," said Joshua.

"Will you go to church with me Sunday?"

Joshua was silent for a minute.

"Oh... well... I... does it matter?" Joshua said in a nervous tone.

"To me, it does," said Mary. Mary could sense it was a touchy subject with him.

"Well, how about I think about it?" asked Joshua.

"That will be okay," said Mary.

The two continued their conversation and said their goodbyes. They were very excited about their date this upcoming Friday. After the phone call had ended, Joshua pondered the question Mary asked him. Mary laid on her bed pondering the answer Joshua gave her.

The next day of school was a wet one. Joshua received a call first thing in the morning. It was Mary.

"Good morning, sunshine, or should I say, rain? Would you like me to pick you up and take you to school?" Mary asked.

Joshua was shocked that Mary would call him first thing in the morning. He was even more shocked that she was willing to give him a ride to school; his answer was a for sure, "Yes!" After a few minutes of good mornings, he gave her directions to his house. Mary was aware that Joshua didn't have a car just yet, and she also knew that she would be the one driving on their soon-to-be date. Thirty minutes later, Mary pulled up in front of Joshua's house in a red Honda Civic.

"Thanks for picking me up in this weather. I wasn't looking forward to riding my bike in the rain," said Joshua.

"You're very welcome. So how was your sleep last night?"

"Actually, I slept really well. I think talking with you and of course, you agreeing to our date, contributed to the sound sleep I had," Joshua said smiling.

"Um, how was your sleep?"

"Well, I actually couldn't sleep that well. It must have been the excitement I had for our date." Mary laughed.

Joshua's eyebrows raised. "This was going to be a beautiful day," he thought to himself. Mary and Joshua discussed the classes they had and continued on their way to school.

The school day went on. Joshua met new friends including Jake Owens from his third-period science class. Jake was short, wore glasses, and according to some classmates, was not one of the most popular students. This did not bother Joshua.

Although the science fair wasn't until the end of the school year, the science teacher, Mr. Lester, gave all the students an assignment to prepare them for the fair. Each student had to find a science partner for the fair and partner up for the entire school year. After the assignment was given, Joshua and Jake worked together and thought about what they could build and enter. Two of the other students, Logan Ferguson, and his partner, Ricky Pearson, were ready for a little competition. Logan picked on Jake throughout high school, so when he saw Joshua and Jake working together, this was a threat to him.

"Find yourself a new partner there, Jakey?" Logan asked in an immature manner.

"Just ignore him," Jake told Joshua.

"Hey, I'm talking to you, four eyes!" Logan blurted out. Logan moved closer to their workstation.

"You need to answer me when I speak to you," demanded Logan.

The teacher had left the room for a moment, which gave Logan the opportune time to mess with Jake.

"Why don't you leave him alone," Joshua stated.

"Why don't you make me?"

Joshua stood up. "I think it's time for you to leave," replied Joshua, now face-to-face with Logan. Logan smirked.

"Your time will come, pretty boy. And yours too, science freak," Logan said as he walked off.

"Thanks, man," Jake told Joshua.

"Anytime, man. Now let's put our heads together for this project."

As the day continued, Joshua did get to visit with Mary in the halls and during the lunch period. The two were becoming close friends. While visiting, Mary introduced Joshua to her best friend, Michelle Waters. Michelle liked Mary's brother, Benjamin, however, he was oblivious to how she felt about him. Michelle also worked at Charlie's Coffee Shop.

During a break between class, Joshua, Benjamin, Mary, and Michelle were talking in the halls.

"So I hear you're the new guy at the coffee shop?" Michelle asked Joshua.

"I am! I start tonight."

"Well, that's great! We could use someone else with all the fall-favorite drinks our customers are requesting," said Michelle.

"I'm really looking forward to it," Joshua said with confidence as he also glanced over at Mary.

After school, Mary and Joshua headed to Charlie's Coffee Shop to begin their shift together. Joshua was looking forward to having Mary train him, but instead, it was Benjamin. Not that he didn't want Benjamin to teach him, he was just looking forward to having Mary do it.

Joshua was a quick learner. He learned how to prepare hot and cold beverages, such as signature coffees, espresso drinks, and wild herbal teas. He also learned how to make several pastries and how specific types of bread went with different beverages. Joshua loved his job. The only problem the job presented was that he was working with such an attractive girl. And, not just any attractive girl. But an attractive girl who said yes to a date with him.

As the night went on, Charlie's Coffee Shop was coming to a close. The four left to close the store were Joshua, Benjamin, Mary, and Michelle.

"I cannot believe how busy it can get in the evening at a coffee shop," said Joshua.

"No doubtarooni, and it's only Tuesday!" replied Benjamin.

"Wait till this weekend; it is going to be crazy busy. Righty-o, Benjamin?" Michelle said as she playfully pushed Benjamin.

"Crikey Criddlesticks, girl, who are you Pushy-Van-Pusherson?" Benjamin laughed.

"Pushy-Van-Pusherson?" Mary laughed out loud. Everyone started laughing.

Benjamin ended up driving Michelle home as she planned it that way, and Mary brought Joshua home. As Mary pulled up in front of Joshua's house, they sat and talked for a while, getting to know one another more. They talked about favorite foods and favorite music. For Joshua, it was pork chops and soundtracks to movies. For Mary, it was Mexican food and Christian music. They talked about short- and long-term goals. Mary's short-term goal was to be a successful writer. Her long-term goal was to be happily married with several children she could take care of and be a mommy to them. Joshua's short-term goal was to start a business. His long-term goal was also to be happily married with several children. Mary and Joshua both loved kids. Although they did not want to end the conversation, they both knew they had to get up for school the next morning.

"I can pick you up from school until you get your own car if you would like," Mary suggested to Joshua.

"That would be great!" Joshua replied gratefully. "My dad said I need to get a few paychecks first before we go pick out a vehicle."

"I would agree with that," giggled Mary.

Joshua reluctantly opened the car door. "See you in the morning," they both said at the same time to each other. They both laughed. Joshua waved as Mary drove off. It was a memorable night.

The week went fast for the students at James River High. It was Friday night—the big night for Joshua and Mary.

"Calm down, son, you're running around like a chicken with its head cut off," Mr. Carpenter said.

"Dad, I can't find my wallet anywhere!" Joshua exclaimed.

Mr. Carpenter picked up Joshua's wallet off the dresser. "You mean this thing? This thing right here?"

"Thank you!" Joshua was relieved for the moment. "Dad, I hate to ask, but—" Mr. Carpenter placed his hand on Joshua's shoulder. He then put a handful of bills in his son's hand as well as the keys to the car.

"Have a nice time tonight, son," Mr. Carpenter said as his hand touched his son's face. He then walked out of the room. Joshua smiled and immediately called Mary. He told her that *he* would be picking her up tonight. Mary was excited to actually be picked up by her date. Joshua had never been to Mary's house, so she gave him directions to her home.

"Be there at seven-thirty!" said Joshua.

"See you then," Mary said as they ended the call.

Joshua pulled up in a Toyota Prius in front of Mary's house five minutes before seven-thirty.

"Okay, deep breaths," he said to himself.

Joshua took in and exhaled several deep breaths. Five minutes later, Joshua was on Mary's front porch. He knocked. Mr. Underwood opened the door.

"Well, hello there. You must be Joshua," said Mr. Underwood.

"Yes, sir," Joshua replied.

"Come on in. Mary will be down in a minute."

"Thank you, sir." Joshua entered the Underwood's home for the first time.

"So, I've heard a lot about you, Joshua."

"Oh? Good things I hope?" Joshua responded nervously.

"They were good things. You have nothing to worry about just yet," smiled Mr. Underwood. "Let me go check on Mary."

"Well. Hi there, Joshua," Mrs. Underwood said coming out of the kitchen.

"Good evening, ma'am."

"So polite. I like that. Mary said you were a good one. And, you look rather handsome this evening."

Joshua was wearing black dress pants with a long-sleeved blue dress shirt and a black tie.

"Must be going to homecoming with our daughter," Mrs. Underwood continued.

"Thank you. Yes, I'm a little nervous but looking forward to tonight."

Mrs. Underwood smiled.

"Oh, and you look splendid yourself," Joshua informed Mrs. Underwood.

"Oh, well, I'm such a mess with all the baking, but thank you."

"Is Benjamin around?" asked Joshua.

"He's at work tonight, lucky for him. He doesn't do dances."

"That's right. Benjamin did mention that. I think Michelle is working tonight too," Joshua said.

"Oh yes, she is anywhere Benjamin is. That poor boy is clueless when it comes to flirting," said Mrs. Underwood.

"That, I would have to agree with." Joshua and Mrs. Underwood laughed.

Mr. Underwood was upstairs and knocked on Mary's door.

"Mary, honey, Joshua is here." Mary opened up her bedroom door.

"You look beautiful, sweetheart."

"Thanks, Daddy," Mary replied with a smile.

"Your date awaits you downstairs, and he seems like a good man," said Mr. Underwood. "And, you call me if you need me."

"Thanks, Dad," Mary said, giving her father a hug.

Joshua looked up as Mary walked down the stairs. She was wearing a teal dress with her long blond hair running down to her shoulders.

"Wow," Joshua whispered. Joshua's body filled with goosebumps.

"You look… you look amazingly beautiful," said Joshua. Mary smiled.

Joshua handed Mary a bouquet of flowers.

"Wow! How sweet. Thank you so much. They are absolutely beautiful," said Mary.

The two stared into each other's eyes for a moment.

"Ok, you two, time to head out," said Mrs. Underwood.

"Mom, will you put these in water for me, please?"

Mrs. Underwood took the flowers and shooed the two out the door. Mr. Underwood walked down the stairs after seeing the two off.

"She's pretty happy, you know," said Mrs. Underwood.

"I know," Mr. Underwood said as he took a deep breath.

"Now don't you worry, honey. She's going to be just fine," Mrs. Underwood said as she embraced her husband.

Joshua walked Mary to the car and opened the door for her.

"After you."

"Why thank you, kind sir," Mary replied.

"Now what kind of music shall we listen to?" asked Mary.

"I'll let you pick," said Joshua. Mary changed the station to a song by Mercy Me.

"This is soothing. Who is this group?" asked Joshua.

"Mercy Me. One of the best groups out there."

"I like it. It's nice and calming," said Joshua as Mary smiled.

Suddenly, they saw something just ahead of them. The street-lights were flickering as the two pulled up to a strange being in the middle of the road.

A homeless person was sitting on the dark concrete pavement. Joshua and Mary pulled up right behind the person as his back was turned. Joshua turned off the car.

"Should we get out?" Joshua was a little hesitant.

"Yes, let's get out and see if he's hurt," said Mary.

Mary opened up the car door. Joshua then followed and opened up his door. Joshua stood with one foot on the ground and one foot inside the car. Mary started walking toward the man.

"Mary, wait," Joshua whispered.

"Hello? Are you okay?" Mary asked as she crept closer to the sitting man.

Joshua was now side by side with Mary.

"Sir, are you all right?" Joshua asked.

Joshua and Mary stopped in their tracks as the man turned his body, placing one hand on the pavement. He was covered with dirt. He had an unshaven face with raggedy clothes, no socks, no shoes. A pair of broken glasses taped together with no lenses barely fit his face. The man's back was covered in a dark, dirty blanket with several ripped holes. His hair was white, but you couldn't tell.

"He's filthy," whispered Joshua.

"Hel-hello?" said the man.

"Are you okay? What are you doing out here in the middle of the street," Mary asked in a concerned tone.

The man looked up at Mary and Joshua.

"I'm just relaxing, taking in the air," said the man.

Mary had the heart for helping people. She loved volunteering for various reasons throughout the year. She occasionally visited nursing homes to talk with the residents. She was especially fond of helping out with the church and dishing out food for those in need.

"What is your name?" asked Joshua.

"Rogers."

The man started to stand up but stumbled as he arose. Joshua and Mary rushed to help him.

"Well, Mr. Rogers, let's get you out of the street," Mary said as she and Joshua helped the man to the curb.

Mary and Joshua stayed with Mr. Rogers for a while. Joshua had his heart set on homecoming, but Mary was intrigued by the old man. This was not the night Joshua had planned. He was ready for his special date with Mary, but it seemed that his night was in for an unexpected turn.

Mary and Joshua decided to take Mr. Rogers to dinner at a local diner. After a quick prayer, Mr. Rogers started to scarf down his cheeseburger, fries, and a chocolate milkshake. The waiter and staff conversed with one another about the old man's appearance compared to what Mary and Joshua were wearing. Other customers also stared at the odd trio. With the gossiping and staring, it still didn't affect their evening.

After dinner, they went to the local small town department store to pick out some clothes. They even bought a new blanket and pillow for Mr. Rogers. As they walked through the clothing aisles, Mr. Rogers was beside himself. He didn't know what to think. He was very thankful for the generosity and compassion that Mary and Joshua had for him.

"Thank you for all you have done for me this evening," said Mr. Rogers.

"You two must be happy to have each other. Did you two just get married?"

Mary and Joshua looked at each other.

"We are on a date. And we are glad we got to spend it with you," said Mary.

"Yes, this has been a very eventful evening with you, Mr. Rogers," said Joshua.

Mr. Rogers smiled at them both.

"You, two, should be married. You make a wonderful couple."

"Whatever God has in store, you never know," said Mary with a smile.

Joshua's eyes widened, and his mouth dropped. He was surprised she said that. Not necessarily her words about God, but her words about being married. Mary smiled as she picked up his chin to close his mouth.

"God is amazing, and as long as you look to him, you've got to listen carefully with both of your ears. You've got to open your heart fully to him, and he *will* guide your steps in a direction on a journey that will absolutely change your life," said Mr. Rogers.

Joshua listened with intent to what Mr. Rogers had to say, although he would tell himself it didn't mean much to him. It did, however, make him think for a moment—a very small moment.

Mary and Joshua concluded their evening with Mr. Rogers. They found out where he was staying and planned on keeping in touch. As Joshua drove Mary home, Mary was feeding Joshua stories of her family. She mentioned about how her grandma lived in the basement and had this revolting smelly blanket. Joshua didn't know what to think. He wondered why she would talk about such a thing. She eventually fessed up and told Joshua she loved to tell stories.

Pulling up to the driveway, it was time for Mary to turn in and call it a night. Joshua was so nervous he started to sweat. He wanted to kiss Mary but didn't know if it was the right time. It was quiet. Mary stopped talking. She just sat there. Joshua thought this was the right moment. It had to be. He closed his eyes, puckered his lips, and leaned over.

"Whoa! You're going in?" Mary asked surprised.

Joshua leaned back. His mouth dropped. He didn't know what to say or do. Mary took her hand and closed Joshua's mouth. She leaned over and gently kissed him on the lips.

"Good night," she said as she exited the car. Joshua got chills all over his body. This had been the best night ever.

CHAPTER THREE

Mr. Rogers

It was the month of December—one week before Christmas. Considerable changes had occurred since the first of the school year. After several weeks working at Charlie's Coffee Shop, and much deliberating along with a little nudge from Mary, Joshua bought a Honda Civic. Benjamin finally caught on to the never-ending flirting from Michelle, and the two were now dating. Joshua and Mary's relationship continued to grow stronger. The two learned about each other's likes and dislikes. One of the things they had in common was that they both loved to watch reruns of Saturday morning cartoon shows when they were kids; particularly cartoons from the 80's when they were aired. Joshua loved watching *Muppet Babies*, *He-Man*, and *The Littles*. Mary enjoyed *My Little Pony*, *Care Bears*, and *Jem*. Mary admired how Joshua was a kid at heart and how he loved to make people smile. Joshua was fascinated by how Mary cherished writing stories. She also adored helping people and made it a point to impact other people's lives with her love and kindness. Joshua loved this about Mary. Although Mary and Joshua's relationship had developed, there was still a part of each of their pasts that were undisclosed to each other.

With Christmas just around the corner, Joshua was elated. He loved this time of year—the lights, music, the decorations. It was his most favorite holiday. To make things even more pleasurable, it was the first snow of the season.

"I can't believe they didn't cancel schoolski today," Benjamin blurted out to Joshua as he shut his locker.

"Hey, it could be worse. We could be working tonight," said Joshua.

Benjamin gave Joshua a look of death. "I am working tonight!"

"Oh, yeah! I forgot," Joshua chuckled for a moment until he looked over Benjamin's shoulder to see Logan up in Jake's face.

"Let it go, dudeski," said Benjamin.

Joshua walked over to see what was going on.

"Looks like Jakey Wakey dropped his books again," Logan said as he pushed Jake's books from his hands. Ricky stood there laughing.

"Leave him alone, Logan," Joshua demanded.

All the students in the hall focused on the situation.

"What are you going to do about it?"

Jake started to pick up his books. Logan kicked one of the books down the hall. Joshua moved closer to Logan.

"I said leave him alone," Joshua now eye to eye with Logan.

Logan smirked and backed up. Joshua started to help Jake pick up his books. Logan lunged his foot toward Joshua. Joshua grabbed his foot just in time and twisted it, causing Logan to fall to the ground. All the students cheered. Logan immediately stood up in a fighting position.

"Get up, let's go!" he said.

Just as Joshua was about to stand up Mr. Lester, the science teacher, walked up.

"What's going on here?"

"Nothing, Sir. We were just getting ready to go to class," said Jake.

"Well, see to it that you do," Mr. Lester said before continuing down the hallway.

"You'll get yours," Logan mouthed to Joshua as he walked away.

Joshua and Benjamin proceeded to help Jake pick up his books.

"Hey bro-man, you okay?" asked Benjamin.

"Yeah, I'm all right," said Jake.

The three picked up the books when all of a sudden, Jake uttered with laughter.

"What's so funny?" asked Joshua.

"That. Was. Awesome!"

"Yeah, I guess it was a pretty good feeling of adrenaline," laughed Joshua.

"Yeah, that was pretty darn hilariousoni. Give it to me dude-o." Benjamin held out his fist to fist bump Jake. It was an interesting morning for the three friends.

As the school day went on, snow continued to fall; consequently, school closed earlier. It was almost a blessing in disguise for school to close early since Joshua had much to do before his evening with Mary's family. It was the first time he was invited over to the Underwood's house for dinner.

"Are you nervous?" Mary asked Joshua as his fingers tapped the steering wheel.

"Well, no. I've visited your parents several times. I'm just thinking about stuff."

"Hmm. Well, tell me about this stuff you're thinking about," Mary said as she wrapped her arm around his. Joshua loved the attention.

"We haven't seen Mr. Rogers in a few weeks. Just wondering how he is doing," said Joshua.

"You know what? We should invite him over for dinner tonight!" Mary said excitedly.

"Really? Your parents won't mind?"

"I don't think they would. I'm going to call them right now." Mary started dialing.

Joshua drove over to where Mr. Rogers was staying. They found him sleeping in his box with snow covered around him.

"All is a go," Mary chirped.

Joshua and Mary went to talk with Mr. Rogers. He was excited to see them both, and he gladly accepted the dinner invitation. Joshua arranged to pick Mr. Rogers up in a few hours. Mr. Rogers was concerned about his appearance, but it didn't matter to Joshua and Mary. They accepted him just the way he was.

The heavy snow ended early in the evening as the flurries took over. The snow covered ground glistened from the streetlight's luminous glow. The Underwoods were preparing for their guests when the doorbell rang.

"They're here!" Mary said nervously.

"Well, get the door silly," said Mr. Underwood. Mary took a deep breath before opening the door.

"Hi, guys. Come, come in," Mary waved for the two to get in from the cold.

"Thank you for allowing me to join you for dinner," said Mr. Rogers.

"You are most welcome. Now, let's get you guys warm and have some dinner," said Mr. Underwood.

Mrs. Underwood prepared an early Christmas dinner for her guests. She made the main course consisting of a Christmas honey-baked ham accompanied with cornbread dressing. She made heavenly eggs, green bean casserole, stuffed meatballs, mashed potatoes with turkey gravy, corn on the cob, jellied cranberry sauce, buttered rolls, and three kinds of pies, including pumpkin, apple, and mincemeat. The feast was fit for a king.

"Can I say the blessing over this meal?" asked Mr. Rogers. The room was silent for a minute.

"Uh, yeah. Certainly," said Mr. Underwood.

"Thank you, good man," said Mr. Rogers as everyone held hands in prayer.

"Thank you, dear Lord, for this incredible feast before us. Thank you for the friendship with this family. Thank you for the kindness surrounding this table. May each one sitting here be blessed with your love, and may they receive the comfort that was bestowed upon me. Words can never be enough for what you continue to provide us with every single day. Thank you for your forgiveness. Thank you for your grace and mercy. We praise you. We love and adore you. We bless you in your Son's holy name. Amen."

"Amen," said everyone.

"That was just beautiful," said Mrs. Underwood.

"Thank you," Mr. Rogers smiled.

Joshua thought for a moment about the prayer.

"Let's eat!" said Mr. Underwood.

After feasting on their dinner, everyone sampled all the home-baked pies Mrs. Underwood made for dessert.

"So, Mr. Rogers, if you don't mind me asking, are you married? Any kids?" asked Mr. Underwood.

"Oh, that's okay, you can ask," said Mr. Rogers as he wiped the whipped cream from his beard. "I do have a son. I was married, but she's now with the Lord," said Mr. Rogers.

"Oh, I'm so sorry to hear that," said Mrs. Underwood.

Mary and Joshua listened in as they had never asked Mr. Rogers about his family.

"Oh, thank you. I appreciate that. That was a long time ago," said Mr. Rogers.

"Do you stay in contact with your son?" Mary asked.

"I visit him from time to time. Um, do you mind if I use your restroom?" asked Mr. Rogers.

"You sure can. It's around the corner to the left of the hall," said Mrs. Underwood as she gathered up the dishes.

"Here, Mom, I'll help with those," said Mary.

"I can help too," said Joshua.

"Oh, now you sit back down. We women can handle this while you boys visit for a minute," said Mrs. Underwood.

Mary smiled and brushed her fingers across Joshua's hand as he placed the plate back down. Joshua smiled back at Mary. Mr. Underwood watched from a short distance. Mary and Mrs. Underwood cleaned up the table and walked into the kitchen. Joshua had a smile on his face while his eyes were fixated on Mary as she left the room.

"Do you love her?" asked Mr. Underwood.

"I do," said Joshua as he bit his lip.

"Have you told her this?"

"Not yet," said Joshua as he stared at Mary in the kitchen.

"Look at me, son. I know you two have been dating for a few months now. I can see in her eyes that she loves you. I can also see it in your eyes that you love her. If she means so much to you, then I would never let a moment pass by without telling her. I wanted you to know that I'm glad you are in her life and am proud of how you treat her."

Mr. Underwood had been meaning to talk with Joshua for some time and thought tonight would be appropriate.

"Listen, Joshua, I'm not sure exactly where you are with the Lord, but just know, her heart is for him. She loves him dearly and places him above and before anything else. That's how she has learned to live and enjoy life.

"I know," agreed Joshua.

"Mary had been in a rough relationship before, and after that relationship, she gave herself to Christ. Since then, her life was transformed like nothing else. I can tell you that Mary's very content with you. My daughter means the world to me, so be a good listener when she has something to share with you," said Mr. Underwood.

"I will. I... I know she was in a prior relationship last year, but she didn't go into details about it."

"I'll let her tell you when she's ready," said Mr. Underwood.

Joshua nodded in agreement.

"Hey, can I ask you something?" asked Joshua.

"Certainly," Joshua whispered into Mr. Underwood's ear, and just as he was finishing, Mr. Rogers walked into the room.

"Well, continue talking. Don't let my presence deter you from finishing your conversation," said Mr. Rogers. The three gentlemen smiled.

As the evening came to a close, the Underwoods offered Mr. Rogers a place to stay for the night, but he graciously declined. Since he decided to head back out in the cold, the Underwoods gave him some thick blankets to keep warm.

"Merry Christmas to you and your family. Thank you again," said Mr. Rogers.

"Merry Christmas to you as well," said the Underwoods.

Mary and Joshua drove Mr. Rogers to a local shelter for the evening.

"Oh, before I forget, I have something for you both," said Mr. Rogers.

He pulled a small box out of his pocket that was taped tightly shut.

"Now, you cannot open this just yet. You need to put it in a safe place, and when you feel the time is right then you can open it," said Mr. Rogers.

"How will we know when the time is right?" asked Joshua.

Mr. Rogers placed the box in Joshua's hand and closed it with his hand. "You'll know." Mr. Rogers exited the car and whispered to Mary. "Don't give up on him," he said.

Mary smiled and whispered back, "Never."

They said their goodbyes and promised to keep in touch.

After Mr. Rogers had been dropped off, Mary and Joshua were contemplating on what to do with the box. They were obedient in not opening it at this time. They decided to hide and bury the box at a local church by a large oak tree. They used a tire iron from the back of the car to dig a hole. The ground was rather hard due to the cold temperature. They both made a pact not to retrieve the box until they thought the time was right.

"So, I was thinking, in a few years, we might have to get a big house for all our kids," Mary said with a smile watching Joshua dig.

"Oh, really? I thought maybe six bedrooms might do it," laughed Joshua.

"Nope, maybe ten," said Mary as she leaned over and kissed Joshua on the cheek.

As the two continued digging, Mary decided to ask Joshua the same question that had been asked several times before, hoping now for a positive response. So she just went for it.

"Wanna come to church with me Sunday? It's our Christmas production, and I know Pastor John would love to meet you. Then after church, a few of us are going to a nursing home to deliver gifts and cook for the elderly. So, I'd like for you to come and be my Christmas church date," Mary said excitedly.

Joshua knew Mary loved helping people and she had asked him several times already to come to church. He could tell she would not let this go and he wanted to do anything to make her happy. Joshua loved Christmas music and decorations so he thought this was a win-win.

"Yes, my sweet Mary. I will come to church and the nursing home with you this Sunday."

"You will?" Mary asked, overjoyed at Joshua's response.

"I will."

Mary looked at Joshua with happiness as he continued to cover the hole. She reached up and moved his hair that had fallen in front of his face so he could see.

"Mary, I have to tell you something," Joshua said as he finished covering up the hole.

Mary sat back in the snow. "Yes, my handsome boyfriend?"

Joshua paused for a moment and looked up into Mary's eyes.

"Mary. I lo—" Just as Joshua started to speak, headlights flashed on the two.

"You two shouldn't be out here this late," said the gentleman from the car. It was Benjamin.

Mary and Joshua stood up. "You scared us!"

"Sorry, sis, I just got off work and saw Joshua's vehicle and thought to myself, 'Hey self, that's Joshoroni's car.' So I pulled on over to see what you two lovebirds were doing."

"You're a dork," said Joshua.

"Come on, let's go," said Mary.

Benjamin ended up giving Mary a ride home since it was getting late. Joshua drove home alone, giving him time to think about his life.

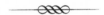

It was Christmas time! Christmas time also meant Christmas break for the students. The past weekend, attending church and helping out at the nursing home was a hit. Joshua had not been to church for some time but did enjoy the time with Mary. Joshua's parents had attempted to get him to come to church several times, but he always declined.

After Joshua and Mary had Christmas dinners with their families, they wanted to share a special Christmas together alone. But first, they wanted to visit Mr. Rogers and give him a gift. They pulled up to the corner of the street to find that his box was gone.

"Excuse me?" Mary asked another man nearby. "Do you know what happened to Mr. Rogers?"

"No, I'm sorry, I don't. I just got here a few days ago. There was no one else here when I arrived," the man replied.

Mary and Joshua asked several other people in the area and local shelters if they knew where Mr. Rogers was. No one recognized Mr. Rogers name, so they didn't know who they were asking about. Mary prayed he was okay.

"He's going to be okay," said Joshua.

"I know he is."

"Maybe he just moved on and found a better place to stay," said Joshua.

"Maybe," sighed Mary as Joshua wrapped his arms around her.

"What will we do with his gift then?" Mary placed the wrapped gift on her lap as she ran her hand across the top.

"Well, let's save it for next time we see him."

"Okay," whispered Mary.

"Come on, I want to take you somewhere." Joshua grabbed onto Mary's hand and led her to the car.

The two arrived at the local park to walk the trails together. Mary thought it was very romantic. Light snow was falling as the two held hands and strolled through the snow talking. After walking their route, they sat at the park bench nestled next to one another.

"Close your eyes," Mary said.

"What are you up to?" Joshua asked.

"I want to give you your Christmas gift. Now close 'em," demanded Mary.

Joshua closed his eyes as Mary placed a necklace around his neck. It was a cross made out of three nails.

"Merry Christmas, babe! I hope you like it."

Joshua lifted the necklace up in his hands.

"I do. I like it very much. Thank you," Joshua muttered.

"Now, it's your turn. Close your eyes."

Joshua reached into his coat pocket.

"No peeking now!" Joshua placed a box in Mary's hands.

"Merry Christmas!" he said.

Mary's eyes opened and lit up. She bit her lip, smiled, unwrapped the tiny bow, and opened the box.

"It's a promise ring," said Joshua.

Mary gleamed with joy as a tear ran down her cheek. Joshua wiped the tear away. He placed the ring on Mary's finger.

"I promise to be yours and yours only. I promise to be faithful to you. I promise to love you because I do. I do love you, Mary. From the first day I met you, in my heart I knew," said Joshua.

Mary hugged and kissed Joshua. She put her hands on his face.

"I love you too," she said.

The two held each other as the snow continued to fall from the starry sky.

"I have something else for you," Joshua whispered in Mary's ear. "Let's go," he said.

The two went back to Mary's house. Joshua rang the doorbell.

"Why are you ringing the doorbell, silly?" asked Mary.

"Just hold on."

Mr. Underwood opened the door with a box in his hands.

"Come in, come in," he said.

Mr. Underwood had Mary sit on the couch and placed the rather large box in her hands.

"Quick, quick! Open it," he said.

Before Mary could open it, the lid popped off. A small bark came from inside the box.

"Oh. My. Gosh!"

"It's a Sheltie. A Shetland Sheepdog puppy," said Joshua.

The puppy was reddish brown with big brown eyes and a giant red bow around her collar.

"How did you do this?"

"Well, I talked to your parents about it, and they agreed on letting me get you a puppy for Christmas."

"I absolutely love her, honey. Thank you so much. This has to be one of the best Christmases ever!"

"Well, what are you going to name her?" asked Mrs. Underwood.

Mary thought for a moment.

"I think, I think I will call her Blankets," said Mary.

Everyone looked at each other. "Blankets it is," said Joshua.

Christmas was coming to a close. Joshua said his goodbyes, kissed Mary, and headed home. Mary told her parents about the promise ring. Joshua told his parents. Joshua and Mary did not think they were rushing into anything. It was a promise ring. It was not an engagement ring. It was not a wedding ring. It was a promise ring of love. Both Mary's and Joshua's parents were accepting about the ring. They knew that even though Mary and Joshua met each other only four months ago, they knew they loved each other deeply.

Later that evening, Mary called Joshua.

"I wanted to call you and tell you again that I had a wonderful Christmas today," said Mary.

"I did too," said Joshua.

"Can I ask you something?"

"Anything," said Joshua.

"Remember that night we buried that box, and you were going to tell me something? Were you going to tell me you loved me that night?"

Joshua thought for a moment. "I thought about it, but I wasn't going to tell you that just yet."

"Oh, well, what were you going to say to me?" asked Mary. Absolute silence was on the other end of Mary's line.

Joshua tried to play it off. "You're just gonna have to wait," he said in a singsong voice.

"Joshua Allen Carpenter! Just for that, you're not getting a kiss for twenty-four hours.

"I think I can wait twenty-four hours."

"Hey!" Mary said, surprised. She thought for a moment. "Well, never mind that. I don't think I can wait twenty-four hours."

Joshua laughed. "I love you, Mary Grace Underwood," Joshua whispered over the phone.

Mary sat there in silence for a moment. Joshua waited for a reply. She smiled an enormous smile and whispered back, "And I love you, Joshua Allen Carpenter."

CHAPTER FOUR

Revealing The Past

The school year was coming to a close, and the twenty-third annual science fair competition was underway. Joshua and Jake completed their project and developed a device called, MDFA—Motivational Displays for Autos. It was compared to digital billboards you saw on the road, except it was for automobiles. The bright LED lights showed motivational text for other drivers who might be having a bad day. One display, in particular, would read, "Slow down. Everything will be all right." It was a warning sign to remind people to slow down as well as a sign for people to let them know their day could get better.

"Nice contraptionski you got there," said Benjamin.

"Yeah, it's kind of cool," Michelle agreed as she held onto Benjamin's hand.

"Thanks, man! But I can't take all the credit. This guy right here created the majority of the machine." Joshua patted Jake on the back.

"Thanks. Thanks, Joshua," said Jake.

Joshua looked around the cafeteria. "Hey, have you guys seen Mary?"

"Last I saw her, she was talking with Mr. Lindwell," said Michelle.

Mary was visiting Mr. Lindwell in the principal's office, discussing her future in writing. She had been in his class her junior year.

"I see great potential in you, Mary. Do not let anyone tell you differently. If you believe it in your heart that your purpose in your life is to write and inspire others, then that right there is what you should do. Those little whispers that you hear telling you to do it, listen to them. And above all, always remember to put God first in all you do, and he will direct your paths. Keep praying. Pray fervently to him and never lose hope. And lastly, keep your faith high and your courage strong, and you'll do well."

Mary always loved when Mr. Lindwell would speak. She loved his words of wisdom.

"Thank you. Thank you again for all your help," said Mary.

"Keep hold of Joshua too. He's a great guy and a pretty decent writer himself," said Mr. Lindwell.

"I will," Mary said as she headed toward the science fair competition.

Meanwhile, Logan Ferguson and Ricky Pearson were presenting their project to the judges.

"What we have here is the wave of the future," Logan said in an arrogant tone. Ricky gave a wicked grin as he nodded his head.

"It is called, the Hand Helicopter," said Logan.

It indeed was an incredible machine. It was similar to a drone; however, it was intended for a person to be airlifted rather than the drone itself. It had two large propellers attached to each end of a long bar. There were also two glove-like devices at the end of the bar which one's hands fit into. One of the devices looked like a motorcycle throttle which was used to accelerate the propellers.

"Does it work?" asked one of the judges.

Logan slipped his hands into the gloves and held on to the bar. He flipped the security button off, turned on the machine, and accelerated the throttle. The propellers spun rapidly, allowing Logan to barely lift off the ground. He turned his hands forward to allow him to move forward. Logan then drove the propellers backward to allow him to go back. He then decelerated the throttle which brought his feet to the ground. The entire room was in awe.

"Very impressive!" said the judge. "Very impressive!"

Joshua and Jake watched on as Logan and Ricky finished their presentation.

"Well, we gave it our best," said Jake.

"Yes, we did," Joshua agreed.

The science fair ended with Logan and Ricky winning first place. Nick Matthews and Jeff Trickle won second place, while Joshua and Jake took third.

"Well, looks like you two just didn't have it in you. Too bad the school year is ending because I sure will miss pushing you around," Logan chuckled.

Joshua and Jake ignored Logan as they continued to pack up their project.

"Whoops!" Logan pushed Jake's paperwork off the table. Ricky did nothing except laugh like he always did.

Joshua walked up to Logan. "What you gonna do, boy?" said Logan.

"Nothing," said Joshua as he looked past Logan, at Mr. Lester.

"Always causing trouble, aren't you Mr. Ferguson?" Mr. Lester led Logan and Ricky to the principal's office.

Mary, Benjamin, and Michelle walked over to help clean up. "I'm proud of you, big boy," Mary said in a different tone.

"For what?" Joshua asked as he turned around, not realizing it was Mary talking to him.

"Well, hi, babe." Mary put her arms around Joshua and looked him in the eyes.

"Well, first for winning third place. And second, for keeping your cool around Logan and Ricky."

"I guess I see no point in putting myself in a position that will cause another problem," said Joshua.

"That is deepinski man," said Benjamin. Everyone laughed.

Graduation day had come! This year had flown by for the students at James River High, and what a year it was. It was a tough year. There were still some big decisions to be made by the graduating class of 2009.

"Joshua, you about ready?" shouted Mr. Carpenter. No answer was given. Mr. Carpenter knocked, then opened Joshua's door.

"You okay, son?"

Joshua looked at himself in the mirror. "What am I going to do with my life now?"

"Well, first things first, let's get you graduated." Mr. Carpenter helped Joshua with his tie.

Mrs. Underwood walked in.

"Wow! My baby boy looks so handsome." Mrs. Carpenter placed her hands on Joshua's face. Joshua pushed them away.

"Mother!" Joshua groaned.

"Oh my, look at the time. Let's go you two. We don't want to be late." Mrs. Underwood had patted Joshua's back before she left the room.

"Son, I wouldn't worry about the unknown. The Bible says—"

Joshua rolled his eyes as he interrupted his father. "I know. I know what the Bible says." Joshua let out a big exhale. "Let's go, Dad."

The graduation ceremony was about to begin. The Carpenters found seats next to the Underwoods. The two families stayed in contact with each other since Mary and Joshua started dating. Mary, Joshua, Benjamin, and Michelle took their seats as the commencement began. The dean gave an inspiring speech to the graduating class as they listened intently to the powerful words spoken. The announcer for the ceremony spouted off the students' names effortlessly. It truly was a memorable day.

After graduation, everyone met outside to congregate. Friends said their goodbyes and disclosed their plans for the future. A few, however, had no idea what to expect or what they would be doing. Joshua was one of those people. He knew one thing, and one thing for sure was that more than anything, he wanted to be with Mary. He had an unforgettable year with her and didn't want this feeling to end or change.

"Hey, man, I wanted to tell you thanks again for being a great friend this school year. I'm really very glad we met," said Jake.

"Hey, no problem. We will definitely keep in contact with one another."

"I have to say since the science fair competition, I have not had any trouble from Logan or Ricky, which is very, very nice," Jake said as he high-fived Joshua.

"That's awesome, man. I think Mr. Lester had some words with them, which, I expect, helped. Let's hope we don't run into them anytime soon."

"Well, I'm off to college next fall, so I might be in the clear. Are you going to go to college?" asked Jake. Joshua thought for a moment. "You know, I'm really not sure, but I did plan on taking a break from school for now."

"I think I know one reason you might be sticking around," Jake smiled as he nodded toward Mary who was coming up from behind Joshua.

"You take care, man," Jake said as he gave Joshua a hug then walked away.

"Hello there, graduating senior at James River High," Mary said as she wrapped her arms around Joshua's neck.

"Hey there, my beautiful graduating girl at James River High," Joshua kissed Mary.

"Hot doggedy, we did it!" bellowed Benjamin as he and Michelle moseyed on over to meet up with Joshua and Mary.

"You are a nut," said Michelle.

"Yes, you are a nut!" agreed Joshua.

The four friends talked about future plans as the day was coming to a close. Joshua and Mary had discussed going to a local college, but neither committed to applying to any university at this time. Mary was very interested in writing classes and thought about taking a few courses to sharpen her skills at being a writer. Although she was interested in writing, her dream was to be a stay-at-home mom.

Joshua wanted to take a few courses to gain some insight on starting a small business. It was Joshua's hope that Mary would want to be a part of this adventure, so they could work together as business partners. For now, he was happy working with Mary at the coffee shop.

Benjamin and Michelle both decided to stay local and go to the same college next fall. It was affordable, and both of them were getting serious as well.

It was graduation night, and it was hopping at Charlie's Coffee Shop. It was a high-traffic hangout place for many students when the school year ended.

"Joshua, can you come in here for a moment?" Charlie motioned Joshua to his office.

Joshua finished the warm caramel, chocolate-drizzled cappuccino for his customer before heading into Charlie's small cornered room.

"Yes, Sir? Did I do something wrong, Sir?"

"No. No. Come in here please and have a seat." Joshua slowly sat down next to Charlie.

"First, congratulations on your graduation today."

"Thank you, Sir. I appreciate that."

"Second, I know you've talked a bit about possibly going to college. Have you made up your mind just yet on what you want to do?"

Joshua fiddled around in his seat, wondering if he was going to be let go. He worked hard and always did right by his customers. What would happen if he was let go? Would he go to college then? What about Mary? So many questions popped into his head, he started to stutter in his response. "I... I... don... don't really know, Sir. I plan on staying here for a while. At least for now," Joshua regained his composure.

"Good," Charlie slapped his thighs as he stood up from his chair. "How would you like to be my assistant manager?"

"Assistant manager?" Joshua questioned in surprise.

"Yep. I have been thinking for some time about adding an assistant manager for my business. I'm not going to be around forever, and I like how you work. You're great with the customers. You're always on time, and I have no complaints. However, there is just one concern. If you were to be my assistant manager, I'm going to have to let Mary go. I know you are very close to her, but I couldn't have a manager in a relationship with their employee. I hope you understand."

Joshua looked out toward Mary as she was taking a customer's order.

"Sir, I appreciate the offer, and I would most certainly take you up on it, but I enjoy working here with Mary."

Joshua was almost at a loss for words. He loved working with Mary, but it was also an unbelievable opportunity.

"What about Benjamin and Michelle? I know they plan on going to college in the fall. Do you know if they plan on staying here? Or what are your plans if they leave?" Joshua asked.

"You've got some good questions, Joshua. I have talked with Benjamin and Michelle, and they plan on staying here at least for now. We get in several applications all the time from students looking for work. I think we will be okay. Now listen, why don't you think it over and let me know. I would appreciate it if you would not bring it up to Mary at this time."

"Yes, Sir. Let me think about it and get back to you."

"All right then, Joshua. Now get on out there to our customers."

"Yes, Sir."

Joshua, Mary, and the others finished their shift and closed up the coffee shop. Mary knew something was up because Joshua was in to see Charlie for some time and he was kind of quiet throughout the evening. Benjamin took Michelle home while Mary and Joshua sat on the outside bench to talk.

"So, are you going to tell me what's up?" asked Mary.

Joshua sat there feeling overwhelmed. It was his graduation day; he was offered an outstanding job opportunity, but overall, his entire world was enthralled by his one true love, Mary. He wasn't infatuated with her; he just knew in his heart, she was the one for him. His relationship was healthy with Mary and felt it was time to no longer keep things from her.

So many concerns were circulating in his mind and now this. His current situation just stacked on to another problem he had. He never wanted to keep anything from Mary, except there still was his lingering past he had not told her about. Now, Charlie wanted him to keep another secret from Mary. What happened in his life was devastating, horrific; it shattered his whole world, causing him to hold much anger deep inside him. He was a very reserved person when it came to emotional situations. Joshua sighed deeply and placed his face in his hands. Mary moved in closer, rubbing Joshua's back.

"Hon? What's wrong? Talk to me." Mary lifted Joshua's sad face. A tiny tear fell down his cheek. Mary caught the tear in her hands as it rolled off Joshua's chin.

"Hon, we have been together almost a year, but it feels like I have known you for eternity because of the relationship we have. One thing though that we have not done is prayed together. I know we go to church together sometimes, but I think one of the main things that will hold this relationship together, is prayer. I want to be part of your life in every way. I want us both to be open and honest with each other about anything. You and I should *want* to pray together as an act of obedience, not an act of just because. You mean everything to me," Mary sighed as she held Joshua's face with one hand and his tear in the other. She too started to get emotional as she didn't like to see Joshua hurting.

"I have your tear in my hand, and I'm going to pray over it," Mary said as she dropped her own teardrop. Joshua held out his hand just in time to catch hers.

"Now we can pray over both our tears," Mary said as she took Joshua's hand.

"Okay," Joshua whispered.

Mary leaned in closer to Joshua and began to pray: "Heavenly Father, we come together tonight to pray over our tears, our fears, our lives, Lord. We pray for wisdom and guidance on how to handle everything that is placed before us. We pray for understanding of the trials that are given to us. We pray for peace and comfort in any decision that we make. We pray we can stand tall and stay strong together as a couple and as followers of Christ. We pray for our relationship, and that you can guide our love, keep us pure, and keep you first. Whatever your will is for us, we know it is in your hands, for you know the plans you have for us. We love you and thank you, Lord. In your mighty, mighty name, we pray."

Mary waited to see if Joshua wanted to say anything. He remained silent.

"Amen," Mary said.

"I'm sorry, I was never good at praying. I used to fumble around my words."

"Used to?" Mary asked concerned.

Joshua stood up from the park bench. His hands were sweating, shaking. He was at a loss for words, but he knew in his heart that he needed to tell Mary what had been on his mind for a very, very long time.

Joshua had fallen away from Christ after circumstances in his life altered his faith and shattered his love that he had for God. He struggled with the relationship he had with Jesus and endured so much pain over what happened. His personal relationship with Jesus was gone—non-existing. Sure, he would pray with his parents to bless meals, but it meant nothing to him. The main times he would pray to God would be in pure hatred to him. There wasn't anything or anybody that would change his mind on how he felt. He harbored strong feelings about his past and would never disclose them to anyone, not even Mary. What he was about to tell her would be bits and pieces of his pain he has been going through. When Mary suggested praying, he did it for her not for God. When they would go to church or talk about the Bible, he did it for her. Joshua was unaware that the one thing that he despised is the one thing that could change his life and bring him love like nothing else, not even from Mary.

Joshua swallowed hard as a few more tears fell down his cheek. He sat back down next to Mary and grabbed her hands.

"Mary." Shivers ran throughout his body.

"I… I lost someone who was very dear to me and I… I have never been the same since." One by one each tear continued to fall from Joshua's downcast face.

"My little sister, Amari, was kidnapped about two years ago. We searched forever, trying to find her. We called everyone we knew to see if, by chance, she was over at a friend's house or a family member's house, anywhere. The whole entire town was looking for her, but she was nowhere to be found."

Joshua's heart tightened in his chest; it felt like it was being crushed. He never knew how painful it was to have his heart feel as if it was fading, squeezed inside his body as if someone was driving a nail right through it. He never talked about his sister because of the deep pain he felt two years ago; now it was all coming back. Mary wrapped her arms around him, for she too had felt similar pain from her past. She embraced him as he wept into her arms.

"Hon, I'm right here. I'm right, he—.

Joshua cried out, "We found her. We found her in a river and… and she was gone. It was all my fault. I should never have left her. She's gone!" Joshua wailed out as he gripped Mary tightly toward him.

Mary held Joshua as he continued to let out the significant emotional pain he had concealed since the loss of his sister. He couldn't go into full details of what happened. The hurt was too real, and the pain was very deep. His idea was to forget about what happened and move on. Mary thought differently. She knew how much he was hurting and knew the best thing she could do was to share God's word with him. She helped remind Joshua that he needed to remember Amari, not forget her.

As the evening went on, they both dried up their tears. Joshua eventually told Mary about Charlie's proposal. Joshua was shocked at Mary's response because she had news for him as well. Mary told Joshua about a job position she was offered. She proceeded to tell Joshua that Pastor John offered her a job at the church working with children. Throughout the week, the church was also used as a preschool, and Pastor John needed someone part-time to help with the children. Mary was ecstatic about the position and always had the heart for children's ministry. She told Joshua she would work at the church and take a few writing courses in the fall to keep her sharp.

"When did you hear about the position? We just talked at graduation, and you never mentioned it," said Joshua.

"Well, after graduation, I got a call from Pastor John, and he told me about the position and asked if I was interested. I couldn't resist, so I told him yes. I haven't even told Charlie yet, but since your news about your position came up, now it won't be that bad," said Mary.

Joshua thought about the situation and realized it was wonderful news for her and for him. The only downside was that he loved working with Mary, and now he would see less of her.

"I'm happy if you're happy," Joshua kissed Mary's forehead. Mary smiled, and she *was* happy. Mary was glad Joshua opened up to her and told her about his past. She still had her own past to discuss with him, but with all the emotions that were just released, tonight would not be a good time.

Joshua was amazed by Mary's response. He always knew she was a keeper. Now after opening up to her and seeing how she reacted, he was relieved. Everything started to feel right in his world, except one thing. He knew Mary had a heart for God, but his heart was still hardened over his sister's death.

He told Mary about his past, but never went into exact details about his faith, or lack thereof. Joshua was afraid that if he revealed to Mary his real feelings about God that she might leave him. He read something before about being unequally yoked, and that was exactly what they were together. His thoughts were to continue acting as if he believed, so he could be with Mary.

Joshua drove Mary home as it was getting late. Before Mary stepped out of the vehicle, she looked deep into Joshua's eyes as she had one final thing to tell him that evening.

"Baby, I know it took courage for you to tell me what you said to me tonight. I want you to know that I love you, and I know you have things going on that make you feel like you are just lost. I will tell you from my heart the real peace and comfort that you are longing for can only come from God. I'm looking forward to spending my life with you, even though you haven't asked me yet," Mary said in a silly voice.

"You have a beautiful heart and a gift of helping others. I've seen it. I don't know for sure where you stand with God. But, I do know that I am there for you to pray with you, pray for you, and help you in any way because I love you."

Mary wiped a tear off Joshua's face before she kissed it. She told Joshua she would see him tomorrow before she said her goodbye.

Joshua stayed parked in the driveway after Mary left. He was speechless and didn't know what to think. He had several emotions and thoughts processing in his head. His heart was exhausted. Although it was a very positive evening, he still repressed negative thoughts about God. To him, Mary was the only *thing* that made him feel safe. Joshua didn't know what he would do without her. Her presence was a comfort to him; more so now than ever since he confessed his past to her. In the midst of Joshua's havocked mind and distressed heart, his eyes lit up as he thought about his future with Mary.

Mary was up in her room looking out her bedroom window down at Joshua. As Joshua drove away, Mary knelt down beside her bed, clasped her hands, and began to pray.

CHAPTER FIVE

God's Presence

Throughout the summer, Joshua continued as the assistant manager at Charlie's Coffee Shop. He earned enough money to move out and live in his own apartment. He, however, visited his parents frequently for dinner nights.

Mary, still living with her parents, was enjoying her time working with the children at the church. She was also working on getting enrolled at the local college to take a few writing courses. She and Joshua would see each other most evenings, however, some nights he worked too late and after he was off, he headed straight home to crash. Mary knew how hard he worked and understood he was tired, but she still missed him. There was one thing that she wished would change about Joshua's job. She wished he wouldn't have to work Sundays. Joshua hadn't been to church with her in a long time.

Benjamin and Michelle continued to date and worked part-time now at Charlie's. Both were getting ready to head to the same college full time in the fall. They were also going to live on campus so they could be close to one another.

One hot summer evening, Joshua's parents invited him over for dinner as they hadn't seen him for some time. While twirling his spaghetti, Joshua noticed his mom who appeared to be in a daydream.

"You okay, Mom?"

"I'm fine, dear. I was just thinking about... oh... it's... it's nothing."

Joshua sighed deeply as he looked at his mom. "I told Mary about her." Joshua placed his fork on his plate and lowered his head. Mrs. Carpenter looked up at Joshua.

"You did? When did you tell her?" Mr. Carpenter stopped eating. He knew how Joshua felt about his sister and how he never wanted to talk about her.

Joshua proceeded to tell his parents about his conversation with Mary on graduation night. He told them about how Mary prayed for him and how he felt about it. Although Mr. and Mrs. Carpenter were devastated and heartbroken over the loss of their daughter, they knew that there was only one solution to their pain, and that was the hope they had in Christ Jesus. They continued to dig deep into the word of God, seeking him while Joshua, struggling with pain and hate, turned from the light. They knew how Joshua felt about God and how he would have nothing to do with him. But that evening, while they were on the subject, they saw something in

Joshua. Something they had not seen in a long time. They saw a small glimmer of hope.

Joshua, for the most part, was a good son. He would not curse, drink, or even raise his voice to his parents. He tried to do good things because that is how he wanted to be treated. His parents knew this about their son. Although Joshua and his parents had a great connection, they knew he still did not have a personal relationship with Jesus.

The family continued to talk throughout the evening. They wept over the loss of Amari but rejoiced over the life they had with her. They even talked briefly about prayer and how important it was. Although Joshua didn't care too much about the subject, he still listened. It was getting late and past Mrs. Carpenter's bedtime. She kissed her son and headed off to bed.

"Are you going to stay the night?" Mrs. Carpenter asked as she peeked from around the corner.

"Probably not, Mom. I'm meeting Mary in the morning for breakfast. Then we are going to a baseball game tomorrow."

Mrs. Carpenter smiled. Joshua used to love playing and watching baseball.

"Well, that is really nice to hear. That will be fun for you, guys. Okay, I have to get to bed. Goodnight, you two."

"Goodnight, Mom."

Joshua and his dad continued to talk while Mrs. Carpenter stood around the corner watching her son in a furtive manner. She was happy to see him opening up, talking about faith and praying even though it was a short discussion. Mrs. Carpenter prayed every day for her son and would never give up on him. She knew one day, no matter how long it took, that he would once again give his life and heart to Jesus. Her faith was strong, and Mrs. Carpenter knew in her heart, that with God, all things were possible. She also was very content knowing her son had Mary in his life. She felt the presence of peace surround her body as she looked once more at her family before she went to bed.

The next morning, Joshua drove over to Mary's house to pick her up. Joshua rang the doorbell.

"Good morning, Joshua. Come on in," said Mrs. Underwood. Blankets excitedly ran up to see Joshua.

"How have you been?" asked Mrs. Underwood.

"I've been really good, just busy with work."

"That appears to always be the case with everyone." Mrs. Underwood said as she called for Mary.

"I think she missed you," Mrs. Underwood said as Blankets reached up to lick Joshua's face.

"I think so too. Such a good girl." Joshua continued to love on the crooked-eared red dog.

"Hey, hon. Wow, I think she missed you," said Mary.

Mrs. Underwood and Joshua laughed.

Mary and Joshua enjoyed a small breakfast that morning, then headed to the local baseball game. It was a beautiful day. The sun was shining, and the temperature was just right.

"Hey batter, batter, batter," Joshua said as he took a bite out of his delicious hotdog.

"Boy, you are in a good mood today," said Mary.

"I haven't been to a game in a long time. My team is winning. I'm here with you. I'm pretty happy." Joshua smiled at Mary as he took another bite of his hotdog.

"Strike!" yelled the umpire. The batter gently tapped home plate as he geared up for the next pitch.

"Come on, Barton. One more!" shouted Joshua toward the pitcher.

"And here comes the pitch," said the announcer.

The batter struck the ball as it flew backward, smacking against the cage in front of Mary and Joshua. Mary screamed in fear. Joshua busted out laughing.

"Scared me to death," Mary said as she giggled too.

"That was so funny. You should have seen your face."

"I'll get back at you, mister. You wait and see."

"Strike three!" shouted the umpire.

"Woo-hoo! Way to go, Barton!" roared Joshua.

"You are really getting into this." Mary was happy to see Joshua was enjoying life.

"I feel really great today for some reason." Joshua smiled, then took a deep breath. He thought about his visit with his parents last evening and what they talked about.

"So, you ready to take a few writing courses this fall?" Joshua asked.

"I am. I have been thinking about writing a story that I really think will turn into something good."

"Oh? What's it about?" Joshua asked curiously.

"Well, it is top secret, and I can't tell you just yet," Mary whispered into Joshua's ear.

Joshua leaned over and whispered into Mary's ear.

"I have a secret too, but I'm not going to tell you either," Joshua kissed Mary's forehead.

Mary smiled. "Hmm, well, I guess I'm going to have to wait then. I'm a patient girl."

Mary sat up straight confidently. Joshua smiled, acting as if he was watching the game, glanced over at Mary, smiling.

"Strike!" barked the umpire.

Mary and Joshua laughed together.

Mary stared at Joshua as he finished up his last bite of hotdog.

"Come here." Mary grabbed Joshua's arm and led him under the bleachers.

"Where are you taking me?" asked Joshua in an excited manner.

Mary started to make out with Joshua underneath the bleachers.

"Wow," Joshua said as he was trying to catch his breath.

"Where did that come from?"

"I just really love you, and you make me very happy. That's all." Mary's eye started to water. She held onto Joshua very close.

Joshua hugged her tightly. "I really love you too," said Joshua as he kissed the top of her head.

"Safe!" bellowed the umpire as the runner made it to home plate.

Joshua and Mary both smiled and shook their heads.

"Let's go out on a date tonight," Joshua suggested.

"I thought you had to work?"

Joshua thought for a moment. "Well, Charlie will be there tonight, and he actually told me if I wanted off anytime this week to just ask. Business has been kind of slow but should pick back up in the fall."

"I do have some writing I need to get done tonight. Hmm, I don't know. Let me check my schedule, and I'll have to get back with you," Mary giggled as she couldn't control her laughter.

"Okay, you get back to me then. I suppose I'll just go to work then," Joshua said as he started to walk away.

Mary ran and jumped on his back. "Where you gonna take me?" she whispered in his ear.

The two didn't end up having a date night. They had a date day and night. After the baseball game, they went back to get Blankets and went on a walk together. They then took Blankets to Tonka State Park so she could play in the creek. At the park, there was a gigantic tree that had fallen across the water. Joshua walked across the tree and then climbed up on another tree branch.

"You be careful!" Mary shouted as she watched. Joshua placed his foot on a tree branch, then hoisted himself up to sit on the limb.

"I used to love climbing trees. It's nice to get out like this. This weather, this day, being here with you, it's just perfect." Joshua looked around, amazed by the scenery, he took a deep breath. "I am pretty content right now."

Mary looked up at Joshua and could tell he was indeed content. She sat back on a rock and thought about her life and how happy she was with him. Although Mary felt peace being with Joshua, she still needed to inform him about her past. She had prayed about when the best time to tell him. He needed to know. "Maybe tonight I can tell him," she thought to herself.

"You ready to see your secret?" Joshua asked as he started to climb down the tree.

"Let's go! You're gonna like this." Joshua grabbed Mary's hand and led her back to the car.

"Come on, Blankets." Blankets splashed through the water and followed them.

Mary was trying to get Joshua to tell her what they were going to do that evening, but he wouldn't tell her. "You'll see" was his response every time she asked.

Joshua dropped Mary and Blankets off and told her to be ready in a few hours. Mary was eager to know what he was planning.

Later that evening, Joshua picked up his date. He drove them to their destination. As Mary looked out the window, she realized he brought her to a place she had not been since she was a kid.

"You've got to be kidding me," Mary said as she opened the car door.

"Well, what do you think? You ready to have some fun?"

"*Yes*! I used to come to this place when I was little and loved it. Why haven't we done this before?" Mary was super excited.

Joshua brought Mary to Chuck E. Cheese's. "You know, where it's fun to be a kid."

"I think it's where a kid can be a kid," Mary laughed.

"Who cares, let's go have some fun!"

Mary and Joshua enjoyed a fun-filled night together. They played Skeeball, air hockey, and arcade games, all while enjoying several pieces of a pepperoni pizza. They did nothing that involved stress. No work talk, nothing negative was spoken about. It was a worry-free evening, so far.

After Chuck E. Cheese's, Joshua had another event he planned for Mary. She was very curious what he was planning.

Joshua pulled up to their destination and put the car in park. Mary lowered the car window, stuck her head out as her eyes lit up.

"What is this?" Mary inquired.

There were several bookcases lined, filled with books. A dessert and coffee stand stood smack-dab in the middle of the square. Chairs and loungers were spread throughout the area. There were lampposts situated around the perimeter. People were reading, writing, and relaxing. There was also an area where they could rent a fresh, clean blanket for stargazing. Joshua brought Mary to an outdoor library center. Mary was in heaven.

"This is unbelievable. How did you find out about this place?" Mary asked.

"Well, my original plan was to take you to Chuck E. Cheese's and then on my way home from the ballgame, I saw a sign that read 'outdoor library.' So I checked into it and found out what it was. I really wanted it to be a special day for you."

"It has been," Mary said in a soft tone voice as she looked around at the rows of books.

First, Mary and Joshua grabbed some coffee and a small dessert to share. They both found a book to read, checked them out, and located a perfect sitting area for them both, right under a brightly lit lamppost. As Joshua read his book, Mary couldn't help but notice how handsome he looked. Joshua was really interested in the book he was reading and didn't consider Mary staring at him. She pretended she was reading her book, peeking over the top corner of page one, daydreaming with her eyes fixated on her man. She was deeply in love with Joshua—mesmerized by him. Her smile turned to a deeply concerned look as her eyes lowered toward the ground. She had to tell Joshua everything that had been stirring in the back of her mind. She just never knew the right time. Surely, this was not perfect timing as she didn't want to spoil the evening. She leaned back in her chair and started reading.

As the night carried on, Joshua came to a stopping point in his book. The library was closing, and people started leaving.

"I'll be right back," he said as he jumped up from his chair.

He later returned with a blanket in his right hand and kept his left hand behind his back.

"Honey, the place is closing, shouldn't we go?" Mary asked.

"I talked to the guy and told him I would put the blanket back when I was finished. He was okay with it."

"What are you hiding?" Mary asked

"Close your eyes." Joshua waved his hands in front of Mary's face.

He kissed her on her cheek, opened up her hand, and placed a small red rose he bought from one of the vendors.

Mary opened her eyes to see the delicate, beautiful red rose.

"You are something else." Mary shook her head, then grabbed the blanket and took off.

Joshua ran after her.

"You know, I have to ask, how can you and I have so much love for one another?" Mary asked as she placed the blanket on the warm grass.

Joshua helped straighten out the blanket as they both laid down next to one another.

"For me, I just know that you're the one. When I first saw you and how you flirted with me, I really wanted to get to know you. You intrigued me. The way you looked at me, the way you smiled, you were absolutely stunningly gorgeous. You also have one of the sweetest and kindest hearts of anyone I know. I guess when I saw you and got to know you more and who you were, my heart was drawn to you. I knew I wanted you in my life. What about you?"

"Well, when you walked into the coffee shop that day, I honestly think my heart skipped a beat. Don't laugh because it's true.

And you looked pretty pitiful looking for a donut." Mary smiled as her hand clasped with Joshua's. They both lay there for a moment in silence looking up at the night sky.

"I prayed for someone to come into my life to bring me happiness, and here you are. I never had anyone ever bring me joy like you do." Mary became nervous because she desperately wanted to tell Joshua what had happened to her.

"You okay, hon? You're trembling." Joshua leaned over and wrapped the blanket over her. Joshua looked down into Mary's weepy eyes.

"What is it, babe?" Joshua asked concerned.

She remained still for a moment, breathing heavily. Mary knew in her heart, it was time to tell him. She took a deep breath.

"I want to tell you something, Joshua. Something that has been on my heart for so long. I need you to know what happened to me. You… you mean everything to me, and I was always afraid to tell you because I don't want you to leave me."

Joshua leaned down toward Mary, touching her face softly. "I will never ever leave you."

Mary sat up facing Joshua, holding his hands. She proceeded to tell him everything.

"I wasn't always a Christian. I was shy and kept mostly to myself. A few years ago, I met this guy. He was twenty-one and older than me. I met him right after my sophomore year. He was new in town, and I was looking for attention. We dated for a few months, but he became abusive." Mary covered her face as tears rolled down her cheeks. "He beat me." Mary choked on her next words. "He... he raped me." Uncontrollable tears flowed from her eyes. Joshua sat there motionless. He had never seen Mary like this before and didn't know what to do. He then reached over and held her close, comforting her.

"Honey?" He lifted her head and started wiping the tears away. "It's okay. Everything is okay." Joshua kissed Mary, wrapping his arms around her.

"I'm sorry I didn't tell you sooner. I was so afraid."

"I know. It's okay. I promise." He lifted her head again. "I love you," he said.

"I love you too," she said as she nestled back down into his chest.

Mary proceeded to tell Joshua that the guy who raped her was now in jail, and he had nothing to worry about. Joshua was very understanding and did his best to console her through this emotional time.

She later went on to say how she became a Christian after the incident and had found her best friend, Michelle, who invited her to church. Mary explained that after her life was given to Christ, God transformed her into who she is today. She told Joshua how she felt after surrendering and confessing her sins to God, and that her life has never been the same since.

It was a declaring night for them both. Joshua admitted he was a Christian until his sister's death and how he now struggled to believe in God. He was worried about telling her this because of how she might feel about him but felt he needed to also be honest. It was all out in the open.

"Can I tell you something?" Mary asked.

"Well, of course, you can."

Mary dried up her tears to share how she actually felt when she came to know Christ.

"I know you've been through a lot in your life, and I may not understand how much you have gone through because I haven't been there, but you should know that I will take care of you and love you no matter what. I guess we all experience something in our lives that we just don't understand. We wonder why it happened or what could have been done differently. I had two choices: to not care about anything anymore and stay in pain, or turn to God. I chose God. I needed something in my life to bring me peace rather than destruction. I see in your heart that you are one of a kind. The way you are to me, the way you interact when someone needs help. You have something inside you that is just waiting to open up and do something big. Stop waiting. I know you are still hurting, and you are happy when you are with me, but I can't be the only one to bring you the real happiness you long for."

Joshua lowered his head. Mary leaned down looking him in the eye.

"Whatever you are struggling with, let it go and let God carry your burden. I promise, once you do this, he will give you the peace of understanding, a blanket of comfort and overflowing love that can only come from him. God can close your door of pain and open another one of hope. Just let him. Do you want that?"

Mary grabbed Joshua's hands. He sat there for a moment, not knowing what to say or do. Joshua looked up at Mary and felt peace. Her hands were warm. Her eyes lit up, and this overwhelming calm came over him. He smiled.

"It's time, honey. I can see it in your eyes. I can feel it in your hands. God is calling for you. What is your heart telling you?

"I'm scared of messing up," Joshua said as he swallowed hard.

"I know, babe. But he will direct your paths as long as you seek him. We all make mistakes. You just have to trust him." she whispered.

Joshua closed his eyes, took a deep breath. "I... I do need him," he said as he bowed his head.

Mary closed her eyes and prayed with Joshua, who rededicated his life to Christ that night, beginning his incredible journey of a personal relationship with his Savior. While both of their eyes were closed, Mary felt chills run throughout her body. Joshua felt it too.

"Do you feel it?" she whispered.

Joshua's eyes remain closed with his hands in Mary's.

"What?" he whispered back.

"His presence."

CHAPTER SIX

Strong Faith

The year flew by and into the following spring. Mary had completed a few writing courses in college and also continued working at the church. She kept in contact with her brother, Benjamin, who was still working at Charlie's part-time, and her best friend, Michelle from time to time. She also started writing her novel, although it was moving pretty slowly. Her love for Joshua continued to grow as well as both of their relationships with Christ.

Joshua had also taken a few writing courses with Mary. He was getting into writing as well. He continued to work at Charlie's and found time to take off on Sundays so he could attend church with Mary. His relationship with Christ was overwhelming. He was amazed how his life was turned around after one single event. He thought differently. He felt differently. He also found time to help Mary a Sunday or two a month with the kids at church. His parents were overjoyed to hear the news about their son.

One Saturday afternoon, Mary was working at the church getting things ready for the following week while Joshua went to visit the Underwoods. He visited with them for some time before picking Mary up from the church for the date they had planned.

"What are you up to?" Mary asked as she ate a bite of fish.

"What do you mean? I'm not up to anything. I just like the way you eat your fish," smiled Joshua.

"Well, you are acting kind of fishy."

"Well, we are eating fish, and you are just so beautiful," Joshua stared hard at Mary.

Mary smiled and pulled her hair from behind her head, letting it drop down the front of her shoulders.

"What are you doing tomorrow?" Joshua asked.

"Well, we have church tomorrow morning, then after that, whatever you want to do."

"Okay! After church, I'm gonna take you somewhere. No questions," he said.

"You're taking me to the art walk aren't you?" Mary asked excitedly.

"I said no questions." Joshua told her to eat her fish.

Mary continued to ask questions that evening while Joshua had to say to her many times to stop asking because he wasn't going to tell her.

"You'll just have to wait and see," he said.

The next morning, Mary and Joshua attended the early service at the church. Mary was not scheduled to volunteer, so they wanted to come to the first service because she didn't want to wait any longer than she had to on what Joshua had planned. Mary could hardly keep still and had a tough time concentrating on what the pastor had to say. When the service ended, Mary grabbed Joshua's hand, and they were the first two out the door.

"Okay. Can you tell me now?" Mary asked.

Joshua didn't say anything and led Mary to the car, opening the door for her. Mary continued to ask questions, but Joshua continued to remain silent. He drove them to the park, and in front of them was a picnic basket and a blanket.

"What is this?" Mary asked as a big smile came over her face.

"Come on, honey." Joshua again opened the car door for Mary. He grabbed the picnic basket and a blanket and led Mary hand in hand across the green grass. He spread out the blanket and set out their lunch for them.

"Okay, I have one question you have to answer. Where did the picnic basket come from?" asked Mary.

"I had Benjamin and Michelle get it together for us," Joshua said proudly. Benjamin and Michelle were watching them from a distance to confirm the basket was taken before they left.

"You are something else, and I love you," Mary said.

After Joshua and Mary finished their lunch together, Joshua suggested they play a game and describe what they see in the clouds. The weather outside was perfect.

"I see a turtle," Mary said.

"I see a fox," said Joshua.

"I see a building," continued Mary.

"I see a wooden cross," Joshua pointed out.

"Oh, wow! I see it too," Mary agreed.

"I see a box," said Joshua.

"Where? I don't see a box." Mary looked throughout the sky.

"Right here," Joshua sat up and pulled out a small black velvet box.

Mary sat up. Her eyes lit up and couldn't speak.

"It's a beautiful day to ask a beautiful question," Joshua looked deep into Mary's blue eyes, "to a beautiful girl," he continued.

"Mary, will you marry me?" Joshua said as he opened up the box to reveal a silver ring.

Mary's hand covered her mouth as a tiny tear of joy fell down her cheek.

"Oh Yes! Yes, I will!" Mary said joyfully as she hugged Joshua tightly.

"I love you," she whispered.

"I love you too," Joshua replied back.

"We have some planning to do," Joshua said in a singsong voice.

"Is this real?" she said.

Joshua nodded his head yes as he smiled.

"I know in my heart that I want to spend the rest of my life with you and you alone."

Mary sighed a deep sigh as she smiled ear to ear.

"We have planning to do," she said excitedly.

Joshua smiled. "Yes. Yes, we do."

Over the next several months, Joshua and Mary planned their wedding with the help of Benjamin and Michelle. They picked a date for the wedding to be sometime in the fall. They knew they wanted to be together and didn't want to prolong the inevitable. Joshua and Mary's parents were supportive and ecstatic. Joshua had asked Mary's parents for their blessing and had also informed his parents he was going to propose. Although much planning had already been completed, there was still a lot to do if they were to wed in the fall.

"Are you going to tell her?" Benjamin asked Joshua as he poured coffee for a customer.

"I'm considering it," Joshua replied as he wiped the counter. He placed the towel over his shoulder and thought carefully for a moment.

"I sure wish business would pick up, I'm getting bored," Joshua whispered so customers couldn't hear.

"Well, why do you care-ski if you—" Joshua stopped Benjamin mid-sentence.

"Shh! Keep your voice down."

"I'm just-a saying," said Benjamin.

Later that evening, Joshua had Mary over for dinner and a movie. He had something he needed to tell her but didn't quite know where or how to start.

"That was a fantastic meal," Mary said as she helped clean up the dishes.

"Well, thanks, honey. But, I think I overcooked the chicken; it was too chewy."

"Well, I loved it and thought it was a pretty good dinner you made us." Mary twirled around Joshua in a flirtatious motion.

"You really up for a movie tonight? Maybe we can play a board game instead?" Joshua suggested as he handed Mary the clean plate.

"I'm up for whatever." Mary placed the last dish in the cabinet.

"Hey, what's with you tonight? You okay? Did something happen at work? Come on, come on, you can tell me." Mary playfully threw punches at Joshua's stomach.

Joshua exhaled a deep breath.

"Man, I don't know where to begin," he said.

"Well, start at the beginning," Mary suggested as she took a seat at the kitchen table.

"You always know what to say. Well, here goes, I know we have more planning to do with the wedding, I guess I'm just nervous about what's going to happen after we get married. Where will we live? Do we need more furniture? Should I stay at Charlie's? How are we going to make more money? Should I stay at Charlie's? Maybe I should look for another job and not stay at Charlie's?" Joshua looked up to see if Mary was paying attention. She was. Her head was propped up by the knuckles of her hands smiling at Joshua.

"You know, honey, I say we take it one day at a time. We mustn't worry about tomorrow because tomorrow will take care of itself. If you feel another calling, leading you into something else, then pray about it and ask God for direction. He'll show you. You just have to be patient and have faith. He'll show you what to do."

"Like I said, you always know what to say. And, you're right. God does have his plans. I just don't know if I want to stay at Charlie's. I have prayed about it, but I'm not sure if it's him talking or not. It's difficult to know at times, and I just don't know what to do as a career. How am I going to support us as an assistant manager at a coffee shop?"

Joshua sat there with his hand on his forehead. His fingers looked like whitewood trees prodding through his ruffled brown hair.

"Well, I guess what I would say is to not worry about it now. We are getting married in a few months and to think about a career change now would be too stressful, you know? What do you want to do?"

"I don't know. I have only taken a few college courses, and I have nothing to show for it. There is so much to think about for our future."

Although Mary always maintained a positive attitude and told others to not worry, she was a little concerned based on Joshua's words.

"Are you... are you wanting to put off getting married?"

"No. No, honey, not at all." Joshua put his arms around Mary. "Getting married to you is one thing that is a given to me. I know without a doubt you are to be in my life." Joshua leaned down and kissed Mary's head. "If there was one miracle from God that I knew was from him, it would be you."

You could tell Mary was relieved to hear those words. They were sincere, honest, and of love.

"You know. I'm *not* going to worry about it. I'll continue to remain at Charlie's and whatever comes my way, I'll continue to pray about it and see where God leads me," Joshua said with confidence.

"Now that's my man of faith!" Mary leaned over to kiss Joshua when they heard a knock at the door.

"Who is it?" Joshua asked.

"Please. Please help me," the man said desperately.

Joshua looked through the peephole and saw an unshaven man. He looked sick and weak. Joshua immediately unlocked the door to help the person. Just as he started opening the door, the man kicked it open, knocking Joshua to the ground. Mary rushed to help him.

The man came inside and shut the door behind him. "Give me all the money you have now," he demanded, waving a knife.

Mary helped Joshua to a nearby chair.

"I said, give me your money now," demanded the man again.

Mary grabbed her purse to get out her wallet. The man eyed Joshua's cross necklace Mary gave him.

"Give me your necklace." Joshua reached up and held on to the cross. The man walked closer to Joshua, pointing the knife in his face. "Give me the necklace, now," the man muttered. Joshua looked the man in the eye, gritted his teeth, pulled the necklace from his neck, and handed it to him.

"Here, here's all the money we have. Please let us go." Mary put the money down on the table.

"You don't have to do this," Mary pleaded. The man picked up the money and then eyed Mary's two rings on her finger, her promise ring and her engagement ring.

"Now those," the man said as he pointed the knife at Mary's rings.

"I... I... can't," Mary murmured. The man lunged toward Mary and grabbed her arm. Mary screamed. Joshua jumped up and executed a spinning back kick, knocking the man unconscious. Mary fell to the ground.

"Mary!" Joshua yelled as he dropped to the floor.

"Hon, are you okay?" Joshua moved the hair out of Mary's wet face. "Sweetie, are you all right?" A flashback moment of her past overcame Mary's thoughts. "Mary? Mary?"

Mary was in shock. Joshua held her close and called the police who was there within minutes.

The night was long for Mary and Joshua. They talked with the police for what seemed like hours. Joshua had called Mary's parents to let them know what had happened. They rushed over to comfort Mary while Joshua talked with the police. After Mary's parents and the police had left, Joshua took care of Mary the rest of the evening. He helped her to his bed, kissed her forehead, and then tucked her in. He made a pallet on the floor to sleep next to her.

"Can you come lie by me?" Mary asked.

"Sure, babe." Joshua grabbed his blanket from the floor and lay next to Mary. She turned over and nestled her head into Joshua's white T-shirt, which helped dry up her tears, then drifted to sleep.

The sunlight shined on Joshua's face the next morning, waking him up. Mary was still asleep. Joshua quietly hopped out of bed trying not to wake her. He dressed and then went to the kitchen to make breakfast. He was hoping the smell would wake Mary up, and they did. She walked into the kitchen to find pancakes, fried bacon, scrambled eggs, and a hot pot of coffee waiting for her.

"Well, hey! Good morning, babe," Joshua said as he flipped a pancake over.

"Good morn—I didn't know you wore glasses." Mary noticed Joshua was wearing black framed glasses.

"I don't normally, I usually wear contacts. My eyes aren't so great, and come to think of it, my parents have perfect eyes; not sure how I ended up with horrible vision," he snickered.

Mary looked at Joshua with her sleepy eyes.

"Well, I adore them, and I think you should wear those more often," Mary said as she yawned. Her head collapsed into her hands.

Joshua lifted her head up. "You okay?" he whispered.

"I'm okay."

"Well, good. And, I hope you have an appetite because I made this for you." Joshua placed a smiley-face plate of food in front of Mary. He had cut out three small holes out of the pancakes and filled them with scrambled eggs. Two holes were for the eyes, and one hole was for the nose. He also placed a small piece of bacon for each of the eyebrows and one long piece for the mouth, while drizzling a line of syrup over the mouth for a mustache. Finally, he positioned two small blueberries into the eggs as pupils for the eyes.

"Wow, this is amazing." Mary stared into Joshua's eyes for a moment. "I don't know what I would do without you," she expressed.

"Ditto," he responded.

Joshua fixed Mary a cup of coffee, then sat down on the bar-stool next to her and blessed the meal.

"So... um, you gonna tell me what was that *Karate-Kid* move you pulled last night all about?" Mary asked as she poured syrup on her pancakes. Joshua laughed.

"Well, I had a trainer in Oregon who taught me a few things after... after Amari died. He was a good friend and mentor, but we went our separate ways." Joshua bit his lip, thinking about his past. His fork swirled around in his eggs. "He's doing his own thing now." Mary could tell it was a touchy subject.

"I haven't done something like that in a long time. The thought of you getting hurt, and when he grabbed your arm, I lost it. You're my girl, and it's my job to protect you. No matter what." Joshua gave Mary a half grin.

Mary sat back in her chair and started eating again.

"It's nice," she said as she cut her pancake in two. Mary paused for a moment.

"It's nice to have a protector," she stated. She then nudged Joshua's shoulder with her own.

The two enjoyed breakfast together and thought it would be best not to talk any further about last night's incident.

With the wedding just a few weeks away, Joshua and Mary decided not to take any further college classes. Mary still dabbled around writing her book and continued working with the kids at the church while Joshua was more focused on his job at Charlie's.

Mary and Joshua were relieved when they found out their parents both pitched in to help with a down payment on a home for them as a wedding gift. They were in awe of how things were coming together.

Late one evening, while Joshua was closing up the coffee shop, he encountered an old friend—Mr. Rogers.

"Mr. Rogers! What are you doing here? Where have you been?" Joshua noticed Mr. Rogers looked tired and weak.

"Are you okay?"

"Joshua, it's so good to see you," he said as he coughed several times. "It's just been a long day. I'm doing well. How are you and Mary doing?"

"We are doing very well. Man, it's really great to see you. I know Mary would want to see you. Are… are you sure you're okay?" Mr. Rogers coughed uncontrollably as he tried to speak his next words.

"I am. Listen, Joshua, I'm not going to be around much longer. I'm moving on soon and wanted to see you before I go."

"Wait. What does that mean? Are you sick? Where are you going?" Joshua asked in a panic.

"Really, I am fine, I just have some things to take care of, but I'll be back." Mr. Rogers said as he cleared his throat.

Joshua looked at him reluctantly, trusting his words.

"Man, I can't believe you are here. A lot has happened since we saw you last. I asked Mary to marry me, and we are getting married in a few days!"

"That… that's wonderful, son. You two make a beautiful couple. You two belong together."

"You. You have to come to our wedding! Can you make it? It's this Saturday," Joshua said excitedly.

"You know what, I'll be there," Mr. Rogers said as he patted Joshua on his shoulder.

"That's great! Mary will be so excited to hear that."

Joshua gave Mr. Rogers the directions to the church. They continued to talk a little while longer. He told Mr. Rogers how he rededicated his life to Christ and how much of a different person he was. Mr. Rogers was delighted to hear the good news Joshua had to share.

"Do you have a place to stay tonight?" Joshua asked.

"I do. Thank you. I better get going now. Would you please tell Mary 'hello' for me?"

"I will," Joshua said as he gave Mr. Rogers a hug.

"You have a lot going for you, son. No matter what life throws at you, no matter how bad Satan and this world beat you down with sin and temptation, don't give up. We may never fully understand why things happen, but what we do know is that we serve a God who is bigger than any problem we face. But you have to seek him. You have to surrender to him. You have to talk to him. You have to walk with him. You have to read about him. You have to share what you know about him with others. You have to have faith. You have to believe, and do not be afraid. You have to continuously choose him first above anybody or anything else in this world. You do that, and his presence, his mercy, his grace, his forgiveness, his comfort and peace, his everlasting, beautiful unconditional love will always be with you to guide and direct your paths on a destination that can only come from him. This is his promise."

Joshua nodded his head in agreement and took heart from the inspiring words.

"I'll see you soon, son."

Joshua stood there for a moment, pondering what Mr. Rogers told him. He felt at peace after hearing those comforting words.

Thinking about his life, Joshua then thought about the wedding. He looked up to see the streetlight shining down on his friend.

We'll see you at the wedding!" Joshua yelled.

Mr. Rogers turned around and waved goodbye. Joshua watched as his friend disappeared into the distance.

CHAPTER SEVEN

Enduring Love

"Where is he?" Joshua asked as he looked around the church.

"Who you talking about, dude-roni?" Benjamin asked.

"Just a friend," Joshua said as his eyes continued to search up and down the aisles.

"Listenski, the wedding's about to start. You ready? You gouda? No second thoughtsaroni?" Benjamin asked Joshua as he straightened his tie.

Joshua stared at Benjamin and shook his head.

"Just checking, bro-dude. The best of man has to double checky this stuff."

"Guys, five more minutes," said Jake.

"Man, I'm really glad you got to make it to my wedding. It means a lot."

"I'm delighted you invited me. I wouldn't have missed it. But, I still can't believe you wanted me to be your groomsman," said Jake.

"Well, man, we are friends. Who else would I pick but my science partner," Joshua said as he glanced one more time throughout the church for his friend.

Meanwhile, on the other side of the church, Michelle was helping Mary get ready. Mary chose Michelle to be her maid of honor and asked a long-time childhood friend of hers, Betsy Williams, to be her bridesmaid. Betsy had flown in from Medway, Massachusetts, to help her friend. She had moved right before high school started, and this was the first time they saw each other in a long while.

"Who are you looking for?" Betsy asked.

Mary and Joshua had talked the night before about Mr. Rogers. They both hoped he would make it to the wedding and was concerned about his health.

"I'm just looking for a friend," Mary said.

"Well, I'm right here, so look no further," Betsy said, fixing Mary's train.

"Yeah, and I'm here too, and it's almost time," Michelle blurted out.

There was a knock at the door.

"Sweetheart, you almost—wow! You... you look so beautiful," Mr. Underwood said as he choked on his words.

"Thanks, Dad."

"We'll see you out there," Michelle said as she and Betsy left the room.

Mr. Underwood admired his daughter for a moment. His little girl was grown up. She was moving on to be her own woman. "How could this be?" he thought. He swallowed hard, lifted his head, smiled, and took his daughter's hand as the music began to play.

While the melodious music filled the sanctuary, family and friends stood to their feet while Mr. Underwood led his daughter down the aisle to her soon-to-be husband.

"Who gives this woman to be married to this man?" Pastor John asked.

"I do," Mr. Underwood replied.

Pastor John continued the wedding ceremony as Joshua and Mary held hands. They continued to look into each other's eyes, mouthing words back and forth.

"I love you," Joshua whispered.

"I love you too," Mary whispered back.

As the pastor continued speaking, it was as if Joshua and Mary were in a world of their own.

The couple exchanged their promises to one another, Mary went first, then Joshua.

"I, Mary, take you, Joshua, to be my lawfully-wedded husband. I promise to love you as Christ loves us. I promise to be faithful, obedient, and honor you through good times and bad times and through sickness and health, until death do us part." Michelle handed Mary a Bible. Mary opened it to 1 Corinthians 4–8 and continued with her vow. "I know that love is patient and kind. I know that love is not jealous, it does not brag, and it is not proud. Love is not rude, is not selfish, and does not get upset with others. Love does not count up wrongs that have been done. Love is not happy with evil but is happy with the truth. Love patiently accepts all things. Love always trusts, always hopes, and always remains strong. Love never ends. I promise to love you like that." Mary concluded as she closed the Bible shut.

Joshua took a deep breath, lifted their held hands to his heart, and began.

"I, Joshua, take you, Mary, to be my lawfully-wedded wife forever and always. I promise to love you with all my heart and love you no matter what comes our way. I promise to take care of you, be faithful, and true to you all of our days. I promise to be obedient and work hard to follow Christ's example of what it means to be a Christian in our marriage through all the trials and tribulations that come our way. I promise to be your husband of faith and prayer partner and promise to help shape a foundation of love that only we can build together. These are my promises to you."

Mary and Joshua continued to hold each other's hand as Pastor John continued.

The rings were exchanged, then the final words were spoken, "I now pronounce you, husband and wife. You may kiss the bride."

Joshua held Mary's face as he kissed his wife for the first time being married.

"Ladies and gentlemen, I now present to you, Mr. & Mrs. Carpenter," Pastor John concluded.

Mary and Joshua smiled before their guests as the music cued them to walk down the aisle.

The reception took place for several hours, and it was nice to see several friends there. Charlie was able to close the coffee shop for a few hours, and Mr. Lindwell also made it a point to attend. As the party was coming to an end, Mr. Carpenter and Mr. Underwood came over to Joshua and Mary's table to drop-off the keys to their home.

"I thought it wasn't ready for a few days," Joshua said.

"Well, we pulled some strings and made it happen for you guys," smiled Mr. Underwood.

"We even had some furniture placed in there for you," said Mr. Carpenter.

Joshua and Mary looked at each other in disbelief.

"Thank you so much," Mary said as she hugged her father and father in law.

"Yes, thank you, guys, very much," Joshua said as he joined in.

Joshua and Mary said goodbyes to their family and friends before heading to their new home.

"I can't believe it. We are married!" Mary exclaimed.

"I know. I am just elated. I am very, very happy," Joshua said as he reached over to hold his wife's hand. "I am also very much in love with you. You, you're—" Mary shushed Joshua and whispered to him, "I know."

"This day was the most perfect day I could ever ask for," Mary said, grasping Joshua's hand tighter.

"Same here, hon. Same here."

"Did you see the way Benjamin and Michelle were looking at each other? Looks like they are next," Mary predicted.

"I think you're right," Joshua laughed.

The two remained quiet for a moment when their happiness fell into a gloomy conversation.

"Not to bring up a somewhat sad subject, but I sure hope Mr. Rogers is okay," Mary said.

"I know. I thought he would make it. I don't even know where to look for him now." Joshua sighed.

"Plus, we never even gave him his Christmas gift. Remember?"

"I do," Mary said.

Joshua thought for a moment about his friend. He felt helpless but then remembered.

"The best thing we can do for him is to pray for him," he said. Mary was impressed with Joshua's words.

"I love you," Mary said as they pulled into their driveway.

"I love you too." Joshua leaned over and kissed his wife.

They looked out from the car window to see their long-awaited abode they had been ready for.

As they opened the door to their home, they were greeted by a very familiar face.

"Blankets!" they both exclaimed.

"Look, honey, here is a note from Mom," Joshua began to read.

"Dear kids, although we loved having sweet Blankets over to visit, we thought it would be fun for her to spend the first night with you together in your home. We love you, guys! Love, Mom."

"Well, that was sweet of her," Mary said.

"Yeah, it sure was," Joshua agreed.

"Do you want to stay with us tonight, girl?" Mary asked as she ran her fingers through Blankets soft fur.

"Arf!" Blankets barked.

"Ha-ha! I think she does," Blankets licked the side of Joshua's face.

The wedding day came to an end, and Mary and Joshua were about to begin a new journey in their lives together. It was a day they would never forget. What soon lay ahead is only the beginning of many life-changing events that would happen because two people fell in love. This is their story.

CHAPTER EIGHT

Brokenhearted

"Honey! I can't find my shoe!" Joshua yelled as he searched frantically for his dress shoe. He searched high and low until he located it deep within his closet.

"I found it!" he exclaimed.

Inaudible words mumbled out of Mary's mouth as she brushed her teeth.

"I'm good-looking?" Joshua asked.

"I said, 'I knew you could find it,'" Mary said as she wiped her mouth with her hand towel before kissing Joshua. "'I'm good looking' sounds nothing like, 'I knew you could find it,'" Mary said as she watched Joshua tie his shoe in the mirror.

"Well, it sounded a little like it," Joshua said smiling.

"Hmm."

Mary took one final look in the mirror. "Whoops, I forgot my mascara."

Joshua stood there admiring his wife, yet he was a little annoyed by how long she was taking.

"We are going to be late and won't get a good seat."

"Okay, ready," Mary said as she grabbed her purse and Bible.

Joshua rolled his eyes as he followed Mary out the door.

It was a beautiful spring Sunday drive to church. Mary and Joshua always looked forward to church but didn't like being late. They pulled into the parking lot and heard the worship music had already started.

"I hate being late," Mary sighed.

"I know!" Joshua grabbed Mary's hand and led them to some available seats.

The two started worshipping with the church to a well-known song they occasionally sang.

Joshua placed his arm around his wife, then kissed her cheek. Mary then leaned over and whispered into Joshua's ear.

"Want a piece of gum?" implying that Joshua's breath smelled bad. He gave her a look, then held out his hand.

After worship, the pastor spoke from the gospel of Mark.

As he was preaching, Mary was distracted by a mother and her little girl who wanted to be held. The little girl looked like she was around five years of age. Mary's eyes then wandered to another family and noticed the father was holding a baby in his arms. She then felt hopeless. She and Joshua had been trying to conceive for over three years now. She had prayed and prayed for something to happen but never received an answer from God. Her faith was still strong, and she knew it wasn't in her timing but his.

Joshua noticed Mary looking at the little girl.

"You okay, honey?" he whispered.

"I'm okay," she whispered back. Joshua knew better.

After service, Mary and Joshua decided to take a stroll through the park. They didn't say much, they just walked hand in hand, watching other parents enjoy time with their kids. They were hoping that one day, God would bless them with a little one.

Later that evening, after dinner, Joshua was helping Mary with the dishes when he was shocked by what Mary had to say. He didn't think he would ever hear her say those words.

"I just don't know if I can continue working with the kids at church. It's just too hard," Mary said as she placed the plate in the cabinet.

"Aw, babe, I know. I'm sure there is a perfectly good reason why it hasn't happened for us yet." Joshua hugged his wife.

"I see the babies and little children in church, and it just makes me sad. They are in malls, grocery stores, schools, parks, foster homes, state care, and even homeless on the streets. Children are everywhere—but here." Mary had taken a deep breath before she continued.

"I always wonder, will I ever be able to make spaghetti necklaces with our own children? Change their diapers? Watch them take their first steps? Will I ever be able to take them school shopping or wave to them as they get on the school bus? Will I ever be able to help them make a Valentine's box or help them with homework? Go to the store and buy crayons and a coloring book for them when they are sick? Will they tell me they don't feel good and ask mommy to take care of them? Will I ever be able to do any of those things?" Mary sighed deeply. "Will I ever get to be a stay-at-home mommy to our children? God, please tell me what your plans are because I'm lost in what your will is."

Mary broke down. The only thing Joshua knew what to do was to comfort her. He carried her into their living room and wrapped her in a blanket and then stroked her hair while she fell asleep on his lap. Blankets could sense something was wrong, so she came over and laid in front of the couch next to Mary. It was a very emotional day.

"What are you working on?" Joshua asked Mary as she tried to cover up the computer.

"What do you think?" she replied.

"Can't I take a peek? I might be able to help," Joshua said in a singsong voice.

Mary gave him a smirk.

"I'm just stuck on how I want my next scene to go."

"Read it to me."

"Well, the part I'm on is about a boy and a girl that met at the beach, and they searched all along the shoreline for seashells. That's about as far as I've gotten."

Joshua looked puzzled.

"What's wrong?" Mary asked.

"It just sounds familiar, like a movie I saw. I dunno."

"Well, you're no help!" Mary grumbled.

Joshua poured himself a cup of coffee.

"How far have you gotten, and how long have you been working on that book? And, aren't you done yet?" Joshua laughed.

Mary wasn't too impressed with Joshua's sarcastic remark. She gave him the evil eye.

"I'm sorry, babe. Will you forgive me?" Joshua leaned down with a pouty look on his face.

"Get out of here," Mary stole Joshua's cup of coffee then playfully pushed him back.

"Hey!" Joshua exclaimed as Mary took a sip.

"I made it for you anyways." Joshua said as Mary took another sip.

"Okay, I'm off to work. Now don't you have too much fun without me, darling."

Joshua drove himself to work, and during his commute, he thought about his life and how happy he was. As he grew older, he had become more of a thinker. Joshua felt as if he was different from other people. While other people were going about their day, he would watch them and see how they reacted to specific situations. Sometimes he would go to a park and sit on a rock just to watch people for hours. Other times, he would open his hands and stare at the lines in his palms just thinking about things. He would open and close his hands and feel how his skin felt as his fingers rubbed together. He thought about his life while doing this and what it was all about. This was calming to him.

Joshua pulled into Charlie's Coffee Shop's parking lot. He still enjoyed working for Charlie. It wasn't his dream job, but he felt blessed to have his job. In the back of his mind, Joshua would occasionally think about other careers that would fit his life. He knew it was in God's hands.

"Joshua, come in here please." Charlie motioned for Joshua to come into his office.

He walked into Charlie's office to see a young, brunette-haired girl.

"Joshua, this is my niece, Avalon."

"Hello there," Joshua said as he shook Avalon's hand.

"Hey," she said back, smiling.

"With Benjamin and Michelle moving on, I mentioned to Avalon we were in need of a couple baristas. She has taken some college courses regarding business and taken some online barista training courses. I think she'll fit right in."

Joshua and Charlie had talked about hiring someone to replace Benjamin and Michelle, but he thought he would at least have some say in the hiring process. She was Charlie's niece, so Joshua couldn't argue.

Benjamin and Michelle both graduated from college, eventually tied the knot a few years after Mary and Joshua were married, and then had recently moved to New York to pursue careers. Joshua and Mary were sorrowful to see their family and friends go, but they knew how happy they were.

"Would you mind showing her around?" asked Charlie. "I've got some errands to run."

"I'm sure Joshua doesn't mind. Do you, Joshua?" Avalon bit her lip as she smiled at him.

"Um, sure. Let's go meet the others," Joshua said in a reserved tone.

"See you later, Uncle."

Joshua introduced Avalon to the crew. He then showed her the different machines and their uses. Avalon, however, was familiar with most of the machines. She wasn't too attentive to what Joshua had to say. She was more interested in Joshua himself.

"So you're married?" Avalon asked.

"I am. Three years now, almost four," Joshua replied.

"Well, she's a lucky girl to have you," Avalon said in a flirtatious manner.

Joshua cleared his throat.

"Well, I'm very lucky to have her," he responded. "She's an amazing wife."

"Listen, I have some paperwork to attend to, so I'm going to have Greg here show you some different coffee concoctions we have. Greg, would you mind showing Avalon a few drink combinations?"

"Not at all," Greg agreed.

Greg was a seasoned barista from Argentina.

"See you later, Joshua. It was very nice to meet you," Avalon smiled and shook Joshua's hand, not letting go.

"It was nice to meet you too, Avalon," Joshua said as he pulled his hand away.

Later that evening, Joshua was working on paying bills in his office.

"Are we ever going to get out of debt? The credit card bills are piling up." Joshua sighed deeply.

Mary was relaxing on the couch, reading a book. She couldn't hear Joshua.

"I'm so tired of working all week and working overtime, then coming home to do bills all the time, finding out we barely have anything left after payday," Joshua raised his voice.

"Are you okay?" Mary asked from the other room.

"No, I'm not! You could help me go through this," Joshua snapped.

Mary walked into where Joshua was.

"Why are you yelling at me?"

"Because, I'm tired after working all day, then I have to come home to this; and you're in there relaxing, and you didn't even have to work today!"

"Well, you didn't even ask me for help."

"I guess I shouldn't have to. If you see me struggling, then you should know to come help me."

"Well, hon, I'm sorry. What can I help you with?"

"Nothing now," Joshua calmly said, sighed then shook his head with a grimace on his face.

Mary walked over to rub Joshua's shoulders.

"Why is life so hard?" Joshua asked.

Mary thought about how they still didn't have a baby to care for.

Joshua got up from his seat.

"What's wrong now?" Mary asked.

"Every time you massage my shoulders, you barely do anything. You rub my shoulders for a minute, then just stop. I thought you were coming over to love on me, but I guess I was wrong," Joshua argued. He stormed into the bedroom and slammed the door. He then came right back out and headed for the front door.

"Where are you going?"

"I just need some time alone," he said as he walked out the door.

Mary didn't know what to think. She stood there confused at what just happened.

Joshua drove around the block and eventually headed into town. While he was driving, he heard ambulance sirens coming from behind him, lights all aglow. He started to say a quick prayer for peace and comfort for whoever was in the ambulance. His mom, when Joshua was a lot younger, always had him pray with her anytime there was an emergency-type vehicle on the road. He couldn't remember the last time he prayed in this situation. He also thought to himself that it was just a piddling little prayer. As the lights sped off into the distance, Joshua pulled from the side of the road to continue on his trip.

While driving, he was listening to Christian music. When he pulled up to a stoplight next to another car who had their windows down, Joshua turned his music down because he felt ashamed of the Christian female artist he was listening to on the radio. He didn't want to be laughed at by the other driver. He always wondered if other people felt the same way he did about this. Joshua thought to himself, "What if he was ashamed of listening to God's music?" He started questioning his faith right there at the stoplight. The light turned green, and Joshua turned the music back up.

As Joshua pulled from the stoplight, he thought to himself once again, "What if the person in the other car needed to hear some inspiring Christian words?" He sighed. It was too late now; they're gone.

Joshua pulled into a local grocery store parking lot to get some snacks. As he walked up to the door, he saw a man sitting on the curb, and he immediately thought about Mr. Rogers. Joshua had not seen Mr. Rogers since the time before his wedding. Mary and Joshua talked about Mr. Rogers periodically and tried to search for him several times, but he was nowhere to be found.

Joshua approached the man, noticed it was not Mr. Rogers, took a step back, turned away, and entered the grocery store.

He walked up and down the aisles and just thought about life and where he was with his life. Joshua also thought about Amari and then started to get depressed. He turned the corner of the aisle when he ran into Avalon, causing her to drop her basket of items.

"Avalon! What are you doing here?" Joshua was shocked to see her.

Avalon bent down to pick up the items, Joshua helped.

"Wow! You scared me! What are you doing here?" Avalon asked.

"I'm just looking for snacks," Joshua replied as he placed a can of coffee in Avalon's basket.

"Buying coffee? That's weird, I think," Joshua smirked.

"Yeah, well, I'm picking up some coffee and items to help me prepare espresso and latte drinks at home so I can practice."

"Oh, well, that's nice. How did you like your first day?"

"Well, I met a wonderful person who was very sweet and helped me out today," Avalon replied.

"Yeah, Greg is a great guy. You can learn a lot from him."

"I was talking about you, silly." Avalon playfully pushed Joshua.

"You know it must be fate that we ran into each other here. I mean, I just met you today, you and I are coworkers, and now here we are at the grocery store. Something's up. Heck, maybe we'll start our own coffee business together." Avalon and Joshua laughed. Joshua pretended as if he was interested.

"Well, hey, I better get going," Joshua said.

"I should go too. I have some practicing to do!" Avalon gave Joshua a smile.

"See you tomorrow, Joshua."

"See you tomorrow, Avalon."

Joshua grabbed the first snack he saw, which was a bag of Oreo cookies, paid the cashier, and left.

When Joshua got home, Mary was in bed, pretending to be asleep.

Joshua was quiet when he moved around the room. He brushed his teeth and got ready for bed.

"Honey?" Joshua whispered as he placed his hand on Mary's shoulder. She turned over and looked into her husband's eyes. Joshua gazed back into his wife's eyes. He took a deep breath.

"I'm sorry for not helping you more with the bills," Mary said as she ran her fingers through Joshua's hair. "I'm also going to pay more attention to your needs and love you more," Mary continued.

"And, I'm sorry too, honey. I didn't mean to get upset with you and storm out like that. It has been a crazy week." Joshua kissed Mary's forehead and held his lips there for a moment.

"I love you, honey," Joshua whispered.

"I love you too, baby," Mary whispered back.

Joshua turned off the lights and snuggled next to his wife. He laid there, thinking about how time goes by so fast and what he could do to be happier with his job and get out of debt. He then thought about how he had a job and how he should appreciate what God has given him.

Mary also had some thoughts of her own. She started thinking about her life too, and how much she loved Joshua. Mary thought about what could be done to bring extra income. She wanted to give up working at the church because it was too difficult for her to be around all the children when she couldn't even have one of her own. Mary knew, though, that her income helped with their finances. She decided to stick with it until God showed her something else. Thinking about the children, Mary then thought about how she still wasn't pregnant. Although aware of other couples who experience infertility, it was still a deep hurt that only she personally felt. She let out a quiet, deep sigh, said a quick prayer to herself while shedding several tears before falling asleep.

CHAPTER NINE

A Glimmer of Hope

The next morning, Joshua woke up to the smell of bacon stirring through his nose. He lay there for a moment, trying to wake up.

"Well, good morning, sleepyhead," Mary said as she walked in, carrying a plate of breakfast food.

"What time is it?" Joshua asked as he stretched out on the bed.

"It's time for you to get up and eat this yummy breakfast," Mary said in a playful manner.

Joshua put on his glasses, then sat up in bed as Mary placed the tray in front of him.

He eyed the platter laid before him. "Wow, this looks great, honey."

Mary sat at the edge of the bed smiling at her husband. Joshua cut into his pancake, lifted his fork to take a bite when he noticed his wife grinning and staring at him.

"What on earth are you smiling about?" Joshua asked as syrup dripped onto his plate.

Mary continued to smile at her husband. Joshua stared back as he raised his eyebrows.

"I've been thinking," Mary began to explain her happiness.

"I know a way for us to make some extra income," Mary continued.

"I'm all ears," Joshua replied.

"Well, I'm only a part-timer at the church, and I thought of another job I could do to help us out."

"I'm listening, babe."

"I could come back to work with you at Charlie's!" Mary suggested.

"You mentioned before you needed someone else, right? I think if we explain to Charlie that our relationship won't interfere with the job, he might be open to it. I believe that it's worth a shot!" Mary exclaimed.

"Well, babe, we already filled that position; or at least, Charlie filled it. He hired his niece to work there. She has some experience and has taken some barista college classes, and that's why he hired her. I really didn't get to have a say-so regarding the hiring process."

Mary sat there disappointed. She thought she had a good idea. She thought about it all morning.

"Well, what's her name? Is she pretty?" Mary asked.

"Her name is Avalon. She just started yesterday."

Joshua didn't mention he saw Avalon last evening at the grocery store. He didn't want to hurt Mary's feelings.

"I didn't ask when she started. I asked if she was pretty."

"Honey, there is only one person that is pretty and beautiful to me and that person is you," Joshua responded with a kiss.

"I have one other thing to say, though. This breakfast is an absolutely fantastic meal, babe!"

Mary felt relieved by Joshua's words.

"I love you," Mary hugged Joshua's neck. Joshua, feeling loved yet choked by Mary's hug, knew of one way to get some relief from the tight hold around his neck. He slowly lifted a piece of bacon to Mary's lips. The hug was released, a bite was taken, and a kiss on the cheek was given.

"I've got to get ready for work," Joshua hopped up out of bed.

"I'm going to think about what else I can do to help our finances," Mary said.

"Babe, I know God will guide us and show us what to do. Just have to trust him."

Mary was amazed to see how her husband had grown closer to God.

She was in a cheerful mood. She started to talk in a baby voice to be cute.

She would mix up her words and act playfully toward Joshua. Joshua was a little concerned.

"Are you okay, honey?" Joshua asked.

Mary was cleaning up the bedroom in a playful manner when she responded, "Do phwhat?"

Joshua laughed to himself. "What?" he asked.

"I'm just euphoric right now," Mary responded.

Joshua was delighted to see his wife in a good mood. Mary had some ups and downs recently regarding the infertility that they were going through. To see her smiling warmed Joshua's heart.

Later that morning, Joshua was working with Charlie on the shift schedule when Avalon walked in.

"Uncle, I need some help with the cappuccino machine."

"Joshua, I think I can finish this up. Can you help Avalon?"

Joshua followed Avalon to the machine to find Greg wiping down the area. A few customers walked into the store.

"Greg, I'm going to help those customers, can you help Avalon with the cappuccino machine?

"Sure thing." Greg was eager to help Avalon because he liked her, but Avalon wasn't interested.

Joshua attended the customers while Greg was trying to show Avalon how to work the cappuccino machine. Avalon, however, was eyeing Joshua and wasn't paying attention.

Lunchtime rolled around for a few of the crew members. Avalon, Greg, and Monique were having lunch outside of Charlie's, at one of the available round tables. Joshua walked out with his lunch to join them.

"You can sit here," Avalon suggested.

Avalon moved over so Joshua could sit by her. He stopped for a minute, exhaled deeply, gave a fake smile, and then took a seat next to Avalon.

While the crew members were enjoying their lunch, Greg told a funny joke which made everyone laugh. It was at this time that Mary had decided to show up and tell Joshua something important. When Mary saw Joshua laughing and sitting next to Avalon, she turned around and headed back to her car. Joshua saw her and followed her.

"Babe? Where are you going?" Joshua asked.

Mary turned around, crying. "Is that her?"

"Honey, I just work with her." Joshua was trying to calm Mary down.

"Why didn't you tell me about her? Why didn't you tell me you hired a pretty young girl?"

"Honey, I didn't want you to worry, and she's just a girl that works with me. You have nothing to worry about."

Mary didn't want to hear anything Joshua had to say.

"I have to go," she said.

Avalon grinned as she saw Joshua and Mary arguing. Mary turned around, walked to her car, and sped away. Joshua was speechless. He didn't know what just happened.

The day continued on. Avalon attempted to comfort Joshua. She sat next to him at the coffee shop counter and put her hand on his back. Joshua could tell Avalon was flirting with him. She told Joshua she would never treat him the way his wife treated him. Joshua immediately got up.

"Avalon, I appreciate your help, but I'm very happy and very much in love with my wife and how she treats me. She means everything to me, and I wouldn't have it any other way."

Joshua walked away while Avalon sat there in amazement.

Later that evening, Joshua arrived home to find Mary curled up on the couch. He tried to call her several times on his way home, but she wouldn't pick up her phone.

"Honey," Joshua said as he sat next to his wife. "Babe, I know how you must feel, but you know me. I love you more than anything. You have absolutely nothing to worry about." Joshua lifted Mary's head, trying to get her to make eye contact with him. "Hon, look at me." Mary raised her eyes to see her husband staring intensely at her.

"I know you've been going through many emotions lately, and I couldn't even begin to understand what you are going through. I know your heart, babe, and how you desperately want a little baby to hold in your arms. I want that too, more than anything. I don't know what God's will is, but what I do know is that you have taught me to believe and put our faith in him. It's in his timing, not ours. These trials we are going through, the ups and downs, will only make us stronger. We have to trust him in everything we do." Joshua placed his hand on the side of Mary's face, pushing her hair back behind her ear. A smile formed on her face.

"I thought about what happened today and what transpired." Joshua paused for a moment. "The devil is the most wicked, nasty, vilest creature that wants nothing more than to destroy our marriage. He wants to attack our relationship and eradicate the love we have for each other. He preys on us, every single day of our lives; but the good news is we have the mightiest Savior on our side, and his name is Jesus."

Joshua leaned over and grabbed the Bible sitting on the coffee table. He turned the pages to Jeremiah 29:11 and began to read. "'I say this because I know what I am planning for you,' says the Lord. 'I have good plans for you, not plans to hurt you. I will give you hope and a good future. Then you will call my name. You will come to me and pray to me, and I will listen to you. You will search for me. And when you search for me with all your heart, you will find me!'"

Joshua closed the Bible, placed his hands onto Mary's and began to pray. Mary felt God's presence as they prayed. She felt his peace and comfort surround her. Mary realized her faith had been slipping away by the doubt of infertility and was overwhelmed by the guilt of not being able to have a child with her husband. As Joshua prayed, she felt happy. She felt content. The display of his love for her opened her heart to believe once again. Her faith was renewed. Her love was restored. A new hope emerged.

------------ ∞ ------------

A few days later, Mary was visiting with her parents while Joshua was at work.

"Mom, do you know of anything I can do to make some extra income?" Mary asked.

"Well, honey, how's your book coming along?" Mrs. Underwood said as she shut the oven door.

"Slow," Mary sighed.

"Dinner almost ready, honey? It sure smells good in here!" Mr. Underwood uttered from the living room. Mary and Mrs. Underwood laughed.

"I'm so glad you brought Blankets over; I haven't seen her in such a long time," Mrs. Underwood said as she poured Mary a glass of sweet tea.

"I think she missed you."

"I think she wants a treat," Mrs. Underwood said.

Blanket's ears perked up.

Mrs. Underwood reached for a dog biscuit and fed it to Blankets as Mary sat thinking.

"Don't worry, honey, something will come up," Mrs. Underwood said.

"I thought about babysitting, but I think that would be too hard," Mary remarked.

"You know, I thought about you the other day, and I meant to call you. Have you and Joshua thought about fertility treatments?"

"We briefly talked about it, but doesn't that cost a lot of money?" asked Mary.

"I'm not sure, but I think it's worth looking into," suggested Mrs. Underwood. "I overheard someone talking about it in the grocery line."

"I'm trusting God knows what he is doing right now," Mary said as she set the table.

"He does, and everything is going to be just fine. Keep strong in your faith and never lose that hope," Mrs. Underwood said as she hugged her daughter.

"Thanks, Mom. Even though I know what I should do, it's always nice to hear it from someone else; especially your mom."

"Well, well, this is what that good smell is?" Mr. Underwood said as he walked into the kitchen.

"Wow, I didn't even have to call you in here, that's a first," said Mrs. Underwood.

"Well, I missed lunch today, so I'm pretty hungry," Mr. Underwood said as he kissed Mary on the head.

Everyone took a seat at the table and held each other's hand as Mr. Underwood blessed the food.

"Dad, do you know anyone that is hiring part-time? I'm just looking for some extra money to help—" Mary stopped in mid-sentence.

"Honey, are you having financial problems?"

"No. Dad, we are just trying to come up with some extra money, that's all," Mary replied.

Mr. Underwood thought for a moment as he buttered his bread.

"You know, I just might have something for you. You know Danny Thompson?"

"As in Danny Thompson Photography?"

"Yes. He is looking for someone part-time to photograph action scenes and comment on the photos and upload them to his blog."

"Oh, Dad, really?" Mary said excitedly.

"What's a blog?" Mrs. Underwood asked.

"Mom, come on," Mary laughed.

Mr. Underwood pulled out his wallet and gave Mary a business card with Danny's number listed.

"He is looking for someone as soon as possible, so give him a call."

"Oh Dad, I will. Thank you!" Mary couldn't wait to tell Joshua.

"Mark, dear, I mentioned to Mary about fertility treatments. Do you know much about them?" Mrs. Underwood asked.

Mr. Underwood looked over at Mary to see her reaction. He knew how Mary felt about the situation and didn't want to bring up any "baby" discussion.

"It's okay, Dad," Mary reassured her father she was all right.

Mr. Underwood let out a deep breath.

"Well, I know it can get pretty pricey, depending on what is done. I definitely would pray about it," Mr. Underwood suggested.

"I will," Mary said.

As the dinner continued, Blankets waited patiently underneath the table for something to fall off someone's plate, a piece of meat, a slice of bread, something. Finally, Mary reached down and gave her a small piece of chicken. You could tell Blankets appreciated the food as she licked Mary's hand. Mary and Blankets were very close. There were times when Mary cried about not having her own baby and always called Blankets her little child. They were inseparable.

Mary visited with her parents a bit longer. While she was there, she called up Danny to see if the job was still available. Danny knew Mary in high school, but he was a few years older. He asked Mary a few questions and offered her the job on a two-week, paid-trial basis since she didn't have any experience. Mary accepted and was very excited about the position. After leaving her parents' house, she immediately called Joshua from her cell phone.

"Honey, guess schwatt?" Mary asked in her baby voice.

"Do you have to be so freaking cute?" Joshua asked.

"Babe, really, guess!"

Joshua thought for a moment. "Um, you had a great time with your parents?"

"Nope. I mean, yes!" Mary responded. "But that's not it. I got a part-time job!" Mary exclaimed.

"Wait, what? How did you?"

"Do you remember Danny Thompson?"

"As in Danny-Thompson-Photography Danny Thompson?"

Mary laughed because she said the same thing.

"Yes! Dad said he was looking for someone to help take pictures, comment on them, and post them on his blog. So I called him up, and he is starting me out on a two-week, paid-trial basis. I start tomorrow!" Mary shouted.

"Wow, babe! That is great news! And, I hate to say it, but the extra income will help a lot."

"I know! And I have some other news that I think we should look into. I want you to keep an open mind, and we will pray about our decision."

"Sure, hon."

Mary pulled into the driveway and opened the garage door.

"I want us to look into fertility treatments and what they are all about. I know we will need to pray about it, but I already feel good about it. I know it will cost money, and I don't know how much, but we will pray about our decision. Okay, honey?" Joshua didn't respond. "Honey?"

Joshua opened the door to the garage and walked out to see his wife. He looked at Mary, smiled, and nodded his head yes in agreement. Mary sat in the car and looked at her husband in adoration. She mouthed three sweet words to him, "I love you." Joshua looked at his beautiful, glowing wife and mouthed those same three sweet words.

CHAPTER TEN

The Prayer Cards

The morning frost outside coated the entire neighborhood. It was the first part of November, and Mary and Joshua just recently had their fourth anniversary. One anniversary gift they gave each other was putting money away in their fertility fund bank—a Cookie Monster cookie jar.

Mary and Joshua saved quite a bit of money over the past few months. Mary had been hired as the part-time photographer for Danny. He really liked her work and her comments on the photos. His blog had more visitors after Mary took control.

With Mary and Joshua both contributing, they were still short on funds to start any treatments soon. However, upon finding out how much Mary and Joshua saved and how much they needed to begin treatments, their parents decided to get together and contribute to help their kids out. They also considered it an anniversary gift.

It was the second week of November when Mary and Joshua started their journey of hope through fertility treatments with Dr. Carol Lynn. Dr. Lynn prepared the couple and explained the process of the treatments. During the treatments, they found out Mary had endometriosis on her right ovary. Dr. Lynn, however, said there still was a good chance to conceive.

The treatments were invasive and involved having Joshua insert a needle into Mary's stomach to inject medication hormones into her body.

After many pills, shots, ultrasounds, and heart-gripping emotions, Mary and Joshua were ready. It was three weeks before Christmas, and their first intrauterine insemination, or IUI for short, was scheduled for eight o'clock tomorrow morning.

The night flew by, and the morning came even quicker. Although Joshua was concerned about the weather, it was still a beautiful sight to see out the Carpenter's bedroom window. The snow was falling heavily outside, coating the ground like a winter wonderland. The inside of their home was also a lovely view. Joshua and Mary decorated their entire house with garland, wreaths, and stockings hung by the chimney. Christmas pinecones were also scattered all over the shimmery tinseled mantel. And to top it off, the seven-foot tall trimmed and beautifully lit Christmas tree was positioned so perfectly in front of the living room window, it caused cars to slow down as they drove by, just so they could catch a glimpse of its beauty.

"Are you ready, honey?" Joshua yelled through the bathroom door.

Mary opened the door wearing a long black dress with tall boots on. Her long, blond, semi-wavy hair canvassed her shoulders. Her blue eyes lit up from the eye shadow she applied. And, she wore just a hint of perfume for her husband. Joshua loved how she smelled with or without perfume, but when she wore his favorite, it drove him crazy for her.

"Wow, babe, uh, you look so beautiful," Joshua complimented.

Mary walked toward him so he could smell her perfume. She wrapped her arms around him, running her fingers through his thick brown hair not saying a word. She just looked at him and smiled.

"We're going to do this, babe," Joshua said.

"I know," Mary whispered.

"You still have the baby name picked out?"

"I do. Can't tell you just yet what her name is," Mary said excitedly.

"Oh, so it's a 'her?'" Joshua questioned. Mary had thought long and hard what she would name her little baby and kept it a secret from Joshua. Joshua didn't mind; he liked a good mystery.

"What a miracle gift it would be to know by Christmas," she continued.

"I know. It seems like this day would never come. God knows what he is doing, we just have to trust him," Joshua responded. Mary and Joshua said a quick prayer and off they went to visit Dr. Lynn for their first IUI.

The first of the year rolled around with no news of a baby for the Carpenters. Although the first IUI failed, Joshua and Mary remained optimistic, and they were already scheduled for their second one in February. With the help of credit cards and some additional money left over from the first IUI, they had just enough funds for another attempt. Their credit cards were maxed out, but they didn't care how much it cost. They had not given up hope.

Even though Mary and Joshua were focused on bringing a baby into their family, their day-to-day routine still existed. Joshua continued to work for Charlie. Charlie, however, mentioned he planned to retire in a few years and wanted to keep Joshua apprised of his plans. Joshua had some interest in buying the place from Charlie, but he was in no position to discuss anything that had to do with finances at this time. His focus, along with Mary's, was to continue treatments. Although Joshua had an interest in buying the place sometime in the future, Charlie had mentioned he would retire but still own the place and make Joshua manager. Joshua enjoyed his job more and more and also was good friends with the employees. Avalon eventually lost interest in Joshua and had moved on to Greg. Joshua was relieved, while Greg enjoyed the attention.

Despite Mary's focus on having a baby, she still found time to work on her book. Mary also enjoyed her part-time job as a photographer-blogger. She continued to use her baby words around Joshua, which always made him laugh. She also was looking for something that she and Joshua could enjoy together and came across a few black-

and-white TV shows that were interesting. She introduced them to Joshua, and as a treat to themselves, they purchased season one of *Leave It to Beaver* on DVD and another DVD with several episodes of *Ozzie and Harriet*. The family-oriented shows were from the fifties, and Mary and Joshua loved them so much they watched them every night before bed. The shows were wholesome. They displayed genuine family virtues. They were addicting to watch.

During the fertility treatments, even though they had one failed IUI, Joshua and Mary's faith remained strong. They leaned on each other for support and became heavily involved with the church. One of their favorite days of the week was Wednesday-night prayer meetings. Prayer meetings consisted of reviewing prayer request cards and praying over them. It was a powerful day of the week for the church. Joshua and Mary both were responsible for handing out the prayer cards to people as they entered the sanctuary. After every person had taken a prayer card, any prayer cards left over would be prayed over together by several church members after church service. There were so many needs, so many prayers crying out for answers. So many people searching for hope. Every Wednesday night, you could sense God's presence flowing through the church.

One evening, while Mary and Joshua were attending a prayer meeting, they handed out all of the prayer cards but three. It was a great turnout that night. To have just three prayer cards left was a great feeling. While service was taking place, Joshua began to read the first prayer card.

The first prayer card request was from a lady who signed her name, Mable N.H. She visited the church a few weeks ago and filled out a prayer card. She lost her husband of thirty years about a year ago and has been depressed ever since. Her late husband was a Christian, and although she wasn't, she didn't know where else to turn but church. It had been a long time since she entered a church, let alone prayed. She also noted that she was recently diagnosed with terminal cancer and had given up on life. She asked for answers. She was looking for hope.

The second prayer card request struck Joshua deeply. It was a young lady who was also dealing with infertility. She came to church one time only because her friend asked her to come. She wrote down on the card she was not a believer but thought it wouldn't hurt to ask someone for answers on why she hadn't been able to conceive. She and her husband had been married for six months and still no baby.

"Six months? We've been trying for over four years!" Joshua thought to himself, still a little emotionally upset about the failed IUI. After he had thought about what he said, Joshua whispered softly to God that he was sorry for thinking such thoughts.

Joshua continued to read the card. The young lady also noted that if there was a God, he would somehow reveal himself to her. She was twenty-three years old; her name was Sarah.

Pastor John continued to read from the Gospel of Luke. It was nearing the time for the congregation to begin praying over the cards.

Joshua quickly started reading the third prayer card. He read the first few lines and then immediately stopped. Memories and flash-backs of his sister, Amari began to affect him. The prayer card wasn't a prayer request, just the opposite. On the card were comments made by a young teenage boy who recently lost his sister and wrote that there was no God, and the only reason he wrote something down was to tell everyone that if there was a God, he would hate him because he let his sister die. It was signed, Lost Soul, brother of Jessica. He wrote P.S. – My parents forced me to come to this dumb church.

The Pastor concluded his sermon and invited the church to begin praying in groups over the cards. Joshua sat there for a moment, holding all three prayer cards barely in his hands.

"Are you okay?" Mary asked.

Joshua gave Mary the prayer cards and walked out of the church into the foyer. She quickly read the cards, then went after her husband. Joshua was sitting by himself, trying to act like he was praying as other church members walked by.

"Honey?" Mary sat down next to her husband.

"What a night, huh?"

Joshua sat there with his hands over his eyes. He said nothing as he tried to wipe away the tears without people noticing him.

"Let's go home, babe," Mary said.

Mary and Joshua headed home after what started to be a blessed evening at church, turned out to be an emotional roller coaster for both of them.

The next morning, Joshua woke up before Mary. Although Mary tried to comfort him last night, he still tossed and turned in his sleep, thinking about Amari. While he was making his coffee, he noticed the three prayer cards sticking out of Mary's purse. She accidentally brought them home, forgetting to turn them in to the church. Joshua began to read them again. As he read each one, he began to pray over them and spent the rest of the morning with God.

Mary awoke a few hours later to find Joshua in the kitchen making notes.

"Good morning," Mary said as she stumbled into the kitchen in her pajamas.

"Hi, honey," Joshua stopped writing to get up and hug his wife.

"Thanks for taking care of me last night. I was a mess, but I've had some time this morning praying, and I think God's telling me to do something about these." Joshua held up the prayer cards to Mary.

Mary sat down next to her husband. She saw the excitement in his eyes.

"I just realized we pray over several prayer cards all the time. We don't really ever know the people, and I think I want to change that. I want to reach out to these people. They need our help." Joshua said.

"How would we know who they are or know how to get in contact with them?" Mary asked.

"Well, this first prayer card, it sounds like she's from a nursing home. Her name is Mable N.H. The only thing I could think was that 'N.H.' stood for 'nursing home.' I was thinking of visiting the closest ones around here and see if we can find her. Her name is Mable, so that might be easy. The second prayer card, she put down her full name as Sarah Campbell. I can look her up on Facebook and see if I could find her."

Mary watched as Joshua continued to express his desire to help these people. After mentioning the second prayer card, he stopped for a moment to see Mary smiling at him. Joshua smiled back. He had a great morning talk with God.

"What about the third prayer card?" Mary asked.

Joshua let out a deep sigh. "I'm going to find that boy too," he said. Mary could tell Joshua was serious and informed him she was there to help him. They both had plans to not only pray over the prayer cards but reach out to the people and share God's love with them. They both realized all the prayer cards had one thing in common—they all needed Christ.

Over the next few weeks, Joshua and Mary continued to investigate the whereabouts of the prayer-card writers. While they had no real leads as of yet, they felt they were getting close. They also had to focus on their fertility treatments—more pills, more ultrasounds, and more shots. Their second and final IUI was a week away. They continued to pray for God's favor to have a child, and Mary became very emotional due to the medication she was taking. She was exhausted, their funds were depleted, it was now or never.

The day before the second IUI, Joshua found Mary writing one evening. She was working on her book.

"Hey, babe, working on your book?"

"I am, and it's coming along quite nicely," Mary said as she confidently finished the sentence she was working on.

"So, are you ever going to tell me what the book is about?" Joshua asked.

"Nope," Mary said with a grin. "You'll just have to wait."

"The last thing you mentioned in the book was about seashells or something like that. So maybe, it's a story about a beach," Joshua guessed.

"I'm impressed you remembered that. Good job, honey, but that's not what the book is about. It is about the beginning of something special." Mary said as she continued writing.

"Oh, that's right, a boy and a girl met at the beach, and they were looking for seashells on the shoreline," said Joshua.

"Getting more impressed," Mary said.

Joshua plopped himself down on the couch. "Seashells, seashells," Joshua thought to himself. "Why do I remember that?" he whispered.

"What did you say, honey?"

"Nothing, babe. I think I'm just super tired." Joshua closed his eyes to nap for a moment.

"Well, we do have a big day tomorrow." Mary closed her computer to spend time with her husband. She noticed his eyes were closed, and she sat there for a moment, admiring him. Mary then had a thought. She turned the lights down low, headed toward the bookshelf, and picked out a record and played a romance dance song. Joshua slowly opened up his eyes to see Mary heading toward him. She reached her hand down, and Joshua graciously accepted the invitation. The music continued as they moved around the room. Joshua held his wife close to him, dancing cheek to cheek. This continued over several songs until they both collapsed on the couch.

"You think it will work this time?" Mary let out a heavy breath. Joshua continued to hold Mary as he thought to himself for a moment.

"Honey?"

"I think God knows what—I mean—I *know* that God knows what he is doing. You and I have been through so many emotions, yet look where we are now. I was lost in my own world until you showed me there is one who will wipe away my tears, take away my fears, and never leave me. It's simply quite amazing how awesome he is." Joshua chuckled as he continued.

"I don't know what will happen after tomorrow, but I do know that God gave me you. I don't know what I'd do if something ever happened to you, hon. So whatever happens after tomorrow, I know I still have you to cuddle with." Joshua snuggled closer to his wife.

Mary felt the stress fall off her as if she had just experienced a day at the beach, sitting in her lounge chair while she listened to the sounds of the ocean waves.

"Plus, I can do this," Joshua slowly dragged his fingers across Mary's side.

"Don't you do it," Mary moved her arms closer to her body.

"Okay, okay."

Joshua listened to Mary, but only for a moment, as he began tickling her. Blankets barked in the background, then jumped on both of them to get in on the action.

"Okay, stop, stop. I'm about to pee my pants," Mary begged. Joshua and Mary both laughed. Joshua moved several strands of hair out of Mary's eyes. She laid there, smiling and out of breath.

"I love you," Joshua said as his eyes surveyed her face.

"Even without makeup and with my hair all ruffled up in my bedclothes?"

"It doesn't matter what you look like. You will always be the most beautiful creature on earth to me."

"I love you so much," Mary said as her eyes wandered over Joshua's face. She leaned up to kiss him and held on until he started laughing.

"I'm sorry, I can't take it anymore. My leg is cramped, and Blankets is not helping." Joshua said.

Joshua pushed himself up from the couch while Mary stretched out her legs. She started laughing.

"What's so funny?" Joshua chuckled.

"My leg was cramping too!" Mary exclaimed. Joshua burst out laughing.

As the night ended, Mary and Joshua went to bed with the hope that tomorrow would be a day for miracles—their miracle.

Three weeks had passed since Joshua and Mary had their second IUI. The procedure went very well, and it was all about waiting now.

They used up all their infertility money from the Cookie Monster cookie jar and had high hopes that this was it.

While they were waiting for their miracle, they continued their search for the prayer card writers. For the first prayer card, they visited several different nursing homes and found a few people with the name Mable but still hadn't found the one who requested the prayer. They still had a few nursing homes to visit before moving to the next town.

Mary continued to search social media for someone named Sarah Campbell to no avail. Out of five local names she found, two were teenagers, one was not married, and the other two were in their sixties. Mary did remember the prayer card mentioning Sarah was married. Although it was difficult to find someone with the last name Campbell, she was not one to give up.

Joshua, although profoundly affected by the last prayer card, remained persistent in trying to find the young boy who lost his sister. The only information he had was the girl's name, Jessica. He googled for answers in his hometown and found nothing. He googled "Jessica's death" and still found nothing. Joshua, like Mary, would not give up until he found who he was looking for. He knew what pain this young boy must be going through and wanted to do whatever he can to help him.

One evening, while Joshua and Mary were working together on finding more information on the prayer cards, Mary had an epiphany.

"You know what?" Mary questioned.

"What?" Joshua responded.

"I can't believe I didn't think of this before." Mary sat in amazement, her mouth open, her eyes were as big as golf balls as she stared into the air.

"I know who Mable is."

"What! How?" Joshua inquired.

"Do you remember when we first met, you finally said yes to coming to church with me, and after church, we delivered gifts to the nursing home? There was a lady who worked there named Mable who was sweet, but wanted nothing to do with Christmas, remember?"

Joshua thought for a moment and remembered the old lady who worked at the nursing home but didn't want to participate in any of the Christmas activities.

"That's her! I do remember."

"Oh, wow! I'm like super excited now! We were looking for someone in the nursing home, not someone who worked there!" Mary exclaimed.

"I can't believe it. I sure hope it's her. I mean 'N.H.' could mean anything. But, for some reason, it struck me as someone from a nursing home," Joshua said.

"Why in the world had we not visited that nursing home yet?" asked Mary.

"Well, we have had a lot on our minds," Joshua replied.

"True. Let's go see if it's her after work tomorrow," Mary suggested.

"Sounds good to me," Joshua agreed.

"I feel different. Like super happy," Mary said.

"Well, you look beautiful," Joshua replied.

"Seriously, I feel different. My body feels different. Maybe I'm pregnant!" Mary joyfully shouted.

Joshua saw the happiness in Mary's eyes. He too felt overjoyed with the hope of their own baby.

"I can't schwait! Maybe I should take a test!" Mary uttered.

"Is it too early? Should we?" Joshua asked.

"Well, we should know in less than a week, and the pregnancy test can predict up to six days in advance!"

Joshua looked at the excitement in his wife's eyes. "Let's do it!" He shouted.

Before taking the test, Joshua and Mary held hands and prayed for God's favor to become pregnant. They knew it was in his hands, yet they hoped for a baby that they could call their own.

After several minutes had passed, while Mary was still in the bathroom, Joshua was becoming impatient.

"Honey?" Joshua knocked on the door. There was no answer.

Joshua opened up the door to find his wife curled up on the floor. He noticed the pregnancy test with the negative sign screeching "failure" at him. He leaned down and sat beside his wife to console her. What was just a happy moment had turned into a catastrophe. Joshua propped his head up against the bathroom tile, trying to hold back the tears to be strong. Mary lay there sobbing in silence as Joshua stroked her hair.

"Where are you, God?" Joshua whispered.

CHAPTER ELEVEN

Lives Changed

The next few months were hard on the Carpenters. With the news of no child yet in their future, Mary and Joshua stepped away from seeking the prayer card writers. They felt it wasn't good timing based on their circumstances.

Mary was devastated, but continued to seek God for answers. She always prayed daily, still hoping there was a chance to bring a little one into the world. She knew though, deep in her heart, it was all in God's timing if it were to happen.

Joshua's faith, on the other hand, had been shaken. He hated seeing Mary hurt and constantly in tears. Many times, Joshua would see Mary praying and crying at the same time, and the only thing he could do was comfort her. He prayed for answers and continued to trust in God but didn't know why things were happening the way they were. They were Christians. They went to church and were obedient. But he could never understand why God wouldn't bless them with a baby.

One late-April evening, Mary and Joshua were visiting Joshua's parents for dinner. It was brought up by Mrs. Carpenter to Mary about possibly having the surgery for the endometriosis. Mrs. Carpenter mentioned she had the same surgery and could give her details of what it entailed.

"I never knew you had endometriosis," Joshua said.

"Well, honey, that's just something we women don't easily share," Mrs. Carpenter said.

Mr. Carpenter didn't say anything as he listened to the conversation. Joshua noticed his movements.

"Dad? You're acting weird," Joshua stated.

"I'm staying out of this one, son," Mr. Carpenter said.

"Mom, did you need surgery before having me or—" Joshua stopped in mid-sentence as he thought about Amari.

The table conversation became silent for several minutes.

"Well, this stuffed-bell-pepper mix is delicious," Mr. Carpenter said, choked up.

Joshua stirred his food with his fork thinking about Amari as Mary rubbed the back of his neck. Mrs. Carpenter closed her eyes, took a deep breath, and continued.

"Sweetie, I had to have surgery to remove the cyst, or else there would have been other problems."

"Well, I think it's something to seriously consider," Mary suggested.

"Are you wanting to have the surgery and then go through another IUI?" Joshua asked.

"Maybe." Mary shrugged her shoulders. "It's worth another shot."

Joshua exhaled a deep breath.

"I'm just worried about you, honey. You've been through so much, and I hate seeing you heartbroken."

Mr. and Mrs. Carpenter looked at each other and smiled.

"We want to help," Mrs. Carpenter said as she grabbed and held on to Mary's hand.

"Mom, no. You guys have already done so much," Joshua responded.

"We won't take no for an answer. We will help you with the surgery and the IUI. There will come a day when you guys will need to take care of us, so in the meantime, we will take care of you."

Joshua and Mary looked at each other and were overwhelmed with support from their parents. They were speechless and graciously accepted the help. The evening was a very remarkable one for Mary and Joshua.

After visiting with Joshua's parents, Mary and Joshua scheduled the surgery with Dr. Lynn for the middle of May. They told Mary's parents, who were excited about their decision. While they waited, life still went on as usual. Joshua still worked at the coffee shop while Mary continued taking photographs and blogging as well as holding her position at the church. She also was getting further along with her book but not as close to finishing as she had hoped, considering how long she had been working on it. Joshua was still a little shaken with his faith over the second failed IUI. He and Mary continued to attend church. There were several weeks where he wanted to just sleep in on Sundays, but Mary urged him always to get up and attend with her.

Before the surgery date, Mary and Joshua planned to make contact with Mable. They wanted to continue their efforts in helping those in need. One late rainy afternoon, they decided to take a chance and visit the nursing home, hoping to find the Mable they had been looking for.

"Wait," Joshua placed his hand on Mary's arm, keeping her from exiting the car. "Stay here."

Joshua exited the vehicle while Mary sat there confused. He opened up Mary's door, holding his jacket over her head so she wouldn't get wet.

"Wow," Mary smiled. "I don't know what I would do without you."

Joshua and Mary entered the nursing home to see several residents either watching out the window, sitting in their wheelchairs, playing games, doing crafts, or some just doing nothing at all. Mary and Joshua looked at each other, shaking their heads.

"Let's go find her," Mary said.

Mary and Joshua went to the front desk to ask the receptionist to see if Mable still worked there.

The receptionist had been working there for a few years but didn't know of anyone named Mable that worked there.

Mary and Joshua were disappointed as they really thought this was it. They thanked the receptionist as they walked away.

"Oh wait," the receptionist yelled.

"Now we do have a resident named Mable. I think Mable might have worked here before, but I'm not sure. I have only been here a few years. Hang on one sec." The receptionist pulled up Mable's chart and had Mary and Joshua sign in before taking them back to see her.

"Mable, I have a few people here to see you," the receptionist said as she opened the door. They found Mable lying on her bed, staring out the window. "I'll leave you two with her."

Mable turned her head to find Mary and Joshua standing there, holding flowers. Mable wore glasses on her craggy face. She wore no makeup. Her hands were wrinkled, folded across each other. Her straight gray hair came down to her shoulders.

"Who are you two?" she asked.

"Hi Mable, my name is Mary, and this is my husband, Joshua. I know this may seem odd, but we are from Heaven's Water Church and did you write this?" Mary nervously asked as she handed the prayer card to Mable.

Mable began to read the card for a moment, then looked up and whispered, "I did."

"Why? How did you find me?" she asked.

"Well, it wasn't easy, but we were determined," Joshua said.

"We are here to pray with you. If you'll let us," Mary said.

"I don't know what to say. I just filled out the prayer card because I was lost. I didn't know what else to do. I was able to come to your church one Sunday, and I only came because my late husband said before he passed that I needed to go with him to church. I never did." Mable dropped her head in shame.

"Hey, it's okay," Mary said as she held on to Mable's hand.

Joshua walked over to the other side of the bed. "Is it okay if we pray with you?" Joshua asked.

"Yes. Yes, of course," Mable whispered.

Mary and Joshua prayed over Mable. They prayed for God's love to surround her. They prayed for peace and comfort with the loss of her husband. They prayed for a miracle healing of her cancer. After the prayer, Mable accepted Jesus Christ as her own personal Savior that rainy afternoon.

Mary and Joshua continued to spend time with her the entire day and, in one visit, changed her life forever. Before Mary and Joshua left, they said they would remain in contact with her and visit her on occasion. They also invited her to come with them to church anytime and stated that they would pick her up if she needed a ride. A friendship was created and for a moment, time stood still in one small nursing room as a new life was born again. After visiting, Joshua felt his heart beat again with joy.

The middle of May rolled around, and Mary's surgery was a success. The cyst was removed which gave Mary and Joshua a better chance to conceive. They had planned to have their third and final IUI in July. If, by God's grace, the IUI would be successful, they would have a child that would be born in the spring of the following year. They knew that it was a long shot, but they also knew God was bigger than anything and could answer prayers.

While they were waiting for their final IUI, they again decided to continue their journey to find the remaining prayer card writers. They had also planned, after finding the last two people, to continue reviewing the other prayer cards that would come in and try to reach out to them as well. Mary and Joshua knew they were on a time clock because when someone is writing a prayer card, they were looking for immediate answers.

One evening, Joshua was working late so Mary decided to pick up a few items at the grocery store.

"Let's see: a loaf of bread, check; tub of butter, check; a gallon of milk, check. Just a few more things for this cake recipe and I'm good to go." Mary was talking to herself, pushing the grocery cart, not paying attention when she struck another person's cart.

"I am so sorry. I was looking at my grocery list and well, I—I am very sorry," Mary apologized repeatedly.

"Oh, it's okay. I wasn't watching what I was doing either. I was looking at my grocery list too," the lady laughed.

The lady was a young dark-skinned tone girl with long brown hair and green eyes.

"It's almost as if they need to have stop signs or signals in here," Mary said as they both laughed.

"I'm Mary."

"Hi, I'm Sarah."

Mary held on to Sarah's hand for a moment with a bewildered look on her face.

"Are you okay?" Sarah asked.

"Yes. Sorry, um, this is going to sound weird, but your last name by chance isn't Campbell, is it?" Mary hesitantly asked.

"Yes. It is. Do I know you?" Sarah slowly pulled her hand away.

Mary was astonished by Sarah's response.

"I can't believe this, but I have been looking for you. I mean, my husband and I have been looking for you." Mary pulled the prayer card out of her purse.

"Did you write this?" Mary asked as she handed the card to Sarah. Sarah looked at the card and didn't understand what was going on.

"How did you get this?" she asked.

"Do you want to get some coffee?" Mary asked.

Mary and Sarah left the grocery store to have coffee together. Mary thought about bringing her to Charlie's but decided she didn't want to be distracted by Joshua, so she went to another local diner.

They talked for several hours as they both had something in common. They both shared stories of infertility, and Mary also went on to share her faith.

"Would you mind if I prayed for you?" Mary asked.

"That would be wonderful," Sarah replied.

Before the night was over, Sarah confessed her sins and gave her life to Christ. She thanked and hugged Mary for everything she had done for her. They exchanged phone numbers and would stay in touch on a regular basis.

When Joshua arrived home, he was hungry and decided to make himself a sandwich.

"Honey? I thought you were going to the store," Joshua shouted as he opened up the fridge.

Mary came around the corner smiling. "You'll never ever guess in a million years who I ran into tonight."

Joshua scratched his head. "I got nothing," he responded.

"Sarah!"

Joshua thought for a moment, "Sarah? Sarah who?" he questioned. "Wait, Sarah Campbell?"

Mary stood there with her arms folded and nodded her head. Joshua listened intently as Mary proceeded to tell him about her encounter with Sarah. The two talked for hours into the night about Sarah, life and a dream to have children together. For in just a few weeks, they would have their answer if they were able to conceive.

July came so quickly. Mary and Joshua headed to see Dr. Lynn to conclude their final IUI. In preparation, Mary had to endure the shots again and emotions that came with it. Although she was excited going through this journey, she was relieved the treatments were complete as she knew this was it. Mary and Joshua talked about In Vitro Fertilization (IVF) but had decided they would accept the final IUI as their answer on whether God wanted them to have a child or not.

Joshua pleaded and prayed desperately as the procedure took place. He held on to Mary's hand through the process, which was not long. After Dr. Lynn was finished, Joshua knelt down and kissed his wife, running his fingers through her hair looking deep into her blue eyes.

"I love you more than anything," he whispered.

"I love you too, honey."

CHAPTER TWELVE

The Struggle

The leaves began to fall as the cold wind blew one late-October morning. Three months had passed since Mary and Joshua found out they could not have a child. Mary had ultimately decided that whatever happened was for a reason, and although they went through several procedures, she knew in her heart that if she were to become pregnant, somehow it was up to God.

She remained in contact with Sarah, who eventually became pregnant. The news of her friend becoming pregnant was a hard hit to the heart for Mary. Hearing her friend talk about the baby depressed Mary even more. Sarah tried to not be overly happy about her baby around Mary because she knew how Mary felt, but it was hard not to express joy over her pregnancy. Although Mary was thrilled that Sarah was pregnant, she was hurt and devastated, but her faith remained strong. If it were meant to be for her to have a child, then she would.

Joshua, on the other hand, accepted the fact that it would never happen for them. He felt like he was a failure and couldn't give his wife a baby. The one main thing Mary had always wanted was to be a mommy.

Over the past few months since the IUI, life at the Carpenters' house had been a struggle. Mary was staying strong the best she could while Joshua felt his past memories creeping up on him. Many arguments took place that had never happened before. It was a hard time for both of them.

"Are you going to come to church with me tonight?" Mary asked.

Joshua laid sprawled out on the couch.

"I'm pretty tired; it's been a long day today."

"Come on, honey. We can both get refreshed after tonight's service."

Joshua let out a deep breath.

"Honey, we go every Sunday. I'm just not feeling like it tonight."

"Sweetheart, I know we have had our share of fighting lately, but I think this might be good for us."

Joshua rolled his eyes. "I just have a question, how are you not upset? I mean, we tried and prayed so many times for a baby and nothing happened. God tells us to ask and it shall be given to us, and it wasn't. I just don't understand how he didn't answer our prayers. We were faithful, we never gave up, we were obedient, and I'd like to think we were good Christians; but *he still didn't bring us our baby*! Don't tell me you aren't mad!" Joshua sat there shaking his head. "You are the strongest and most loving person I know. How? Life is supposed to be joyous and fun, but it seems that if you are a Christian, you have to give up your freedom, and you *might* get your prayers answered. It seems like a lose-lose situation to me. You are an amazingly faithful and obedient woman, but you still don't get your prayers answered? Whatever!" Joshua chuckled.

Mary sat next to her husband. She knew he had been hurting and had bottled up his feelings for a while. "Honey. Joshua? Above anyone else, I understand how you feel about the situation, but we cannot blame God for this. I have always looked at it, that it will always be in his time, his will, not ours. Sweetheart, our treasure is in heaven, not here. You, however, are my piece of heaven here on earth. We have had our ups and downs, trials, and tribulations, but we must never lose sight of how perfect God's grace and love is for us. He knows what is best for us, and he has a plan that is bigger than ours could ever be. We have to trust him, honey. You talk about God answering prayers. Think about what he did for Mable, what he did for Sarah. They both were looking for answers. They are now experiencing a beautiful relationship with Jesus. Their prayers were answered, and we were a part of that. That makes me happy."

Mary and Joshua sat silent for a moment as Mary continued. "Mable is no longer depressed, and we have a great relationship with her. God's not done with her yet, and she is, well, she's content now even in her condition. And although Sarah is pregnant—yes, it hurts more than anything, I mean more than anything—she is excited and has a relationship with God because we did not give up on her. They both do!"

Joshua sat there with his hands over his face, elbows on his knees. Hearing about Sarah getting pregnant angered him even more.

"Well, that's just great. They are happy and have what they want but not me. That seems to be the story of my life, nothing is ever going right, except you. It's as if my life is meant to be miserable. My job sucks, we can't get pregnant, and Amari—" Mary put her hand on Joshua's back to try to comfort him.

"My Joshua, the only thing I know to do is to have faith. I have to believe that God is leading us to a place that can only bring us closer to him. That is what keeps me going. You keep me going."

Mary placed the Bible on Joshua's knee.

Joshua still focused on his life, the infertility situation, and the death of his sister, in anger, picked up the Bible and threw it against the wall.

"I'm not going to church!" he yelled. Blankets ran into the other room.

Mary sat there bewildered at what just happened. She had never seen Joshua act like this. Mary didn't know what to do, so she calmly walked into her bedroom and shut the door.

She leaned her head and hands up against the door, broke down, letting all the built up emotions out and wept uncontrollably.

Joshua could hear his wife's cries as he sat there in great distress. He knew he hurt Mary, but he too was suffering himself. Joshua felt very regretful after throwing the Bible and apologized to God for doing so.

Several thoughts went through Joshua's head as he paced back and forth across the living room floor. He paused for a moment and noticed his Bible spread open, leaning up against the wall. Joshua walked toward the Bible, glaring at it on the ground, bent down as if he was going to pick it up, but then changed his mind. He opened the bedroom door slowly to find Mary lying in a fetal position on the bed. Joshua sat down beside his wife with his hands folded between his knees.

"I'm sorry, honey," he whispered.

Mary reached up, wrapped her arms around Joshua, and held on tight.

"I don't know what to do or how to feel. I'm lost on what I'm doing with my life, and I don't know what is right from wrong at times. I can't be happy, or in a good mood, all the time with our life as it is. It is too hard. It is just too hard."

Mary listened to Joshua as she held on to him. She wiped away her tears, then hopped up, and booted up her computer.

"Come here, honey," she said. Joshua walked over to Mary as she was pulling up images on the computer. "I want to show you something," she said.

Mary pulled up pictures of disasters that had occurred all over the world. She showed Joshua images of tornadoes, hurricanes, wildfires that had destroyed homes and even entire cities. There were images of children crying and sitting amongst the rubble of their once happy home. She then proceeded to pull up several websites of shootings, wars, and other losses that people around the world experienced.

"Why are you showing me this?" he asked.

"Because, sweetheart you are not alone. I know how much you are hurting. More than you'll ever know, I know." Mary held on to Joshua's hands as she looked up at him. "I wanted to show you there are millions of people in the world that are hurting. Millions are lost. I mean really lost, honey. They choose to do things that they feel are right but are of this world, and not doing what they need to do for God's kingdom. This world, this world is a place where life just happens. There will be loss. There will be hatred. There will be hurt, but even though there will be disasters and loss that occur throughout our life, there is also love, hope, happiness, and peace. Life is a roller coaster of emotions that never ends, and although we don't understand it, there's a reason for it all."

Mary exited out of all the images and websites she had pulled up. She then looked up pictures of joyful people and miracles that had happened.

"I'm not saying that whatever we are going through isn't as big as what other people are going through, but I am saying that life will throw us curves all the time. And although there are curves thrown at us, there are also straight lines that lead us down a road filled with smiles, peaceful thoughts, and contentment. Life is what you make it. It's about going through the good times and the bad that makes us stronger inside and who we are."

Joshua stood there listening to Mary's words as she continued.

"I know you're upset about us not having a baby and believe me, I may not show it at times, but I, too, am hurting inside. I, too, cannot understand why it hasn't happened for us, but I need to continue to have faith that God has something better for us. I've been on a few websites and have been reading about what other people have gone through. They didn't have any money and had given up because they couldn't afford it. I don't know their circumstances, but I do know ours. Our parents helped us with a majority of the expenses and some couples don't even have that." Mary grabbed Joshua's hand.

"I know, honey. I hear what you are saying, and you are right. It just seems like life is harder than it is easy. These past few months, I have had several doubts in my head about what it actually means to be a Christian. It's so hard to believe and have faith and trust someone I can't see and yet he isn't answering our prayers. Plus, why would God allow destruction and hatred to take place in this world if he wants us to be happy," Joshua said as he pulled up a chair to sit next to Mary.

Mary got up to sit in her chair backward, to rest her arms on the back of her seat.

"Honey, God doesn't allow destruction and hatred to take place in this world. You keep forgetting there is a devil out there who is taking control of people's lives. He tricks us, follows us, and waits for that exact perfect moment, then attacks us. He is sneaky, tricky, and leads us into temptation and wants nothing more than to destroy any relationship someone has with Christ. He is a deceiver and will blind people's heart from believing in the One who can forgive their sins and show mercy and everlasting grace for each and every one of us. So we need to stand firm and guard our heart and pray, pray, pray. Prayer is so powerful. So powerful." Mary moved her head around so Joshua would look into her eyes.

"Joshua, look at me. You keep telling me I'm strong, and I seem to always have it together, but do you remember those times you prayed for me? Because of your faith and strength, you made me strong. And those times I prayed for you and made you strong. We work together and help each other through the good and the bad. You say we can't see God, but I see him every day when I see you. I see him when I look out into the distance and see what he created."

Joshua placed his head in his hands as he continued to listen to his wife. Mary proceeded to talk to him about faith and what it meant to be a Christian to her.

"You said you didn't know what it meant to be a Christian. Just because you are mad at God doesn't make you an unbeliever. We all have our doubts and our disbelief, but if you continue to trust in him, have faith and pray to him daily, he will show you and give you miracles that can only come from him."

Mary reached down to look Joshua in the eyes to ensure he was paying attention to her.

"And another thing, life is more than understanding what a Christian is; there are so many things that will happen that we will never understand. At any moment, life can change in an instant. We are not perfect. We will get mad. We will have hate in our heart at times. We are all sinners. But while we are all sinners, Christ died for us. Being a Christian means confessing you are a sinner and submitting your life to Christ, and living your life for Christ. It means knowing what he did for you on that cross for your sins, and believing and having faith in him. It's about repenting of your sins and asking for forgiveness and being committed to him by sharing his Word with the lost. It's a transformation, babe, which you will know as the Holy Spirit lives inside you. To sum it all up, it is about having a personal relationship with him always."

Joshua let out a deep sigh. "But I feel like I'm slipping away from him, and it's hard to continue to keep remaining positive right now, let alone trying to *please* him every day. I'm just not strong enough."

"You are strong enough, babe. Just remember when you gave your life to him. Think about what went on inside your heart the moment he came into your life."

The room was silent.

"Are you praying and asking him for help?" she asked.

"He should already know I need help."

Joshua sat there at the edge of his chair, twirling his thumbs. He thought about his past and let negative thoughts consume him even more. Joshua continued to doubt himself as a Christian as he thought about his sins. His mind wandered into reminding him of how he was ashamed of God at times. He thought about how he wasn't perfect and how he had desired to have what other people had.

"Christian. Yeah, I'm a Christian all right. A sinner of Christ is what I am. More like a 'ChristSin.'"

Joshua shook his head in disbelief.

"You hear me, Lord? I'm a Christian all right—a *'ChristSin!'*" Joshua shouted, trying his best to pronounce "ChristSin" as Christian. He shook his head some more and bit his bottom lip as several thoughts raced through his head.

Mary ran her fingers through Joshua's thick brown hair. "You know, honey, the enemy is always there attacking us. Always. He is waiting for the perfect opportunity to bring us down and tear us apart. And, although the enemy is telling us we are no good and trying to destroy us, God is also always there to pick us up, protect us, and hold on to us."

Mary lifted Joshua's head. "He loves you, babe. Don't ever give up on him. Because I promise, I promise he will never give up on you," Mary whispered. "He will show you what to do, just continue to seek him. You have to keep seeking him. Don't lose hope, babe," Mary said as she held on to Joshua's hands.

Joshua was tired of arguing. He couldn't believe how close he was to God, but now he was struggling with what was going on in his life. Although he was worn out, Joshua always loved it when Mary talked to him. He felt peace in his heart as he thought about one good thing God had done, which was bringing Mary into his life. This made Joshua smile to know that he had someone who loves him as much as she did. Although he felt Mary's love surround him, and he still believed in God, he still had reservations about why God allowed painful events to happen.

Joshua hugged Mary and immediately went out the bedroom door to pick up the brown leather-bound Bible and placed it on his nightstand beside the bed. He told her that he felt better and planned on seeking out the young boy from the prayer card. Deep down, he felt this was his purpose and if he could make a difference in the young boy's life, he wanted to try.

Mary prayed over Joshua while Joshua thought about the kid. He was keen to find him and wholeheartedly believed this was his calling. He realized if there was one thing he could relate to, it was what this boy had gone through. And even though these thoughts might have come from God, Joshua never thought if this was God's calling or God's will.

The next day Joshua and Mary decided to take a walk through town. They bundled up as the highs for the day was only in the fifties. They visited several shops and enjoyed their time together, rekindling their relationship after the night they had. They eventually ended up strolling through the park where Joshua proposed. A hotdog vendor was selling hotdogs which was one of Mary's favorite foods. They bought a few dogs, chips, and a couple of pickles, and ate together on a park bench as they people-watched and talked for a majority of the day. It was a day they both would never forget.

Several weeks later, Joshua and Mary were visiting Joshua's parents to find out what other resources could be used to find the young teenage boy they had been seeking. They told them about the circumstances regarding the young boy, and they were proud of Joshua for what he was doing.

"Maybe the church might have some more information on the parents. I never even thought of that," Joshua said as he flipped through old photos of his childhood his mom stored in a shoebox.

"I checked with a couple of the associate pastors when the card was first written, and they didn't know who the parents were," Mary said.

"Figures," Joshua chimed.

"Honey!" Mary exclaimed.

"Well, I thought it was a good idea, and I just mean it figures that it wasn't."

"Keep praying and you'll find him," Mrs. Carpenter chimed in.

"Well, all the leaves are blown away from the doorstep," Mr. Carpenter said as he entered the house.

Everyone laughed at how Mr. Carpenter was dressed. It was freezing outside, and Mr. Carpenter had bundled himself up to keep warm. He was wearing a ski mask with several layers of clothing on.

"Looking good there, Mr. C," Mary said.

"I dress to impress," he replied as he took off his mask.

As everyone continued laughing, Joshua stumbled across a peculiar photograph of an ultrasound.

"Mom, what's this?" Joshua asked as he held the photo up.

Mr. and Mrs. Carpenter were speechless as they looked at each other.

"Um, well, honey, that's a long story," Mrs. Carpenter said.

"What do you mean? Wha—who is this? The photo says 'Baby Carpenter,' and it is dated 1989. That's two years before I was born."

"Dad?" Joshua attempted to get answers.

Mr. Carpenter came over to sit next to Mrs. Carpenter to talk with Joshua. Mary sat next to her husband.

"Well, honey, remember when I said I had surgery to remove a cyst? I was pregnant and carried a child for several months, but there were complications. I had a miscarriage and lost the baby. I found out after the miscarriage that I had a cyst, and then your father and I decided I should have the surgery to remove it."

"Why didn't you ever tell me?" Joshua asked concerned.

"We—" Mrs. Carpenter was interrupted.

"All this happened before I was born and then we lost Amari. What is—is this family cursed or—"

"Joshua. Son, we struggled with the right time to tell you all this, and I don't think now is such a good time," said Mr. Carpenter.

Mrs. Carpenter dropped her head. Mary just sat there trying to figure out what else was going on.

"Is there something else?" Joshua questioned. "Mom? Dad? Tell me," he demanded.

"Honey, after the miscarriage and the surgery, we found out that we couldn't have any children. So… So we checked into what adoption was about."

"What? No… no… no… no way," Joshua said, choking on his words.

"Sweetheart, God brought you to us, and you have always been our son," Mrs. Carpenter continued.

"No! This… This can't be happening."

"Joshua." Mr. Carpenter placed his hand on Joshua as Joshua yanked his arm away.

"You lied to me! All this time, you… you lied to me."

"Honey, we didn't lie to you, we were trying to protect you," Mrs. Carpenter said.

Joshua couldn't believe it. He was shaking, breathing heavily.

Mary was confused. "Amari?"

"We were told we couldn't have children, so we gave up but knew we still wanted children. God brought us Joshua, and then several years later, we found out we were pregnant with Amari. We couldn't believe it," said Mrs. Carpenter.

Joshua started to clench his fists.

"What happened to my parents?" Joshua asked as he gritted his teeth.

The room was silent.

"What happened to my parents?" Joshua demanded an answer.

"They were in an accident when you were just a baby. This was the same time we were looking to adopt, and that's when we found you. We love you so much." Mrs. Carpenter could not hold back her tears. Mr. Carpenter reached over to hold his wife. Mary also held on to Joshua as he couldn't believe it.

"Let's go," Joshua whispered to Mary.

Joshua and Mary grabbed their keys and headed for the door.

"Joshua. Son, please don't go," Mr. Carpenter didn't know what else to say.

"Son."

"Don't!" Joshua shouted pointing his finger at his father before walking out the door.

Mary drove while Joshua sat in the passenger seat trying to process what just happened. More and more, he felt his world being turned upside down. The one main question that kept popping up in his head was, "What's next?"

CHAPTER THIRTEEN

The Promise

Winter was approaching, and over the past few weeks, Joshua had come to the realization that things were the way they were, and he could do nothing about it. He hadn't spoken with his parents since he found out about his adoption and didn't plan on talking with them anytime soon. Although he was hurt about not knowing he was adopted, Joshua felt a little peace knowing that he was wanted.

Mary comforted Joshua over the past few weeks, helping him again with the heartaches and pain he had been going through. She knew he had been through a lot. She also knew she was very lucky to have him in her life to where she could be there for him. Despite all that was going on, Joshua remained very close to Mary. He needed her as much as she needed him.

Joshua searched for information about his birth parents but had no luck. He felt this was a journey he would have to continue until he found out more answers as to what happened. Mr. and Mrs. Carpenter had no information on who his birth parents were because it was a closed adoption. The only information they knew was that his birth parents didn't survive an accident, but they never knew what kind of an accident it was.

After a few hours of internet searching, Joshua decided to take a walk to clear his head while Mary lay in bed. She had been sick for a few days and wanted to rest. It was cold out and snowing, but Joshua still wanted to get out of the house for a while. He strolled by several businesses and found himself walking to various places that he and Mary had visited in the past. Joshua visited the church where they buried the gift they received from Mr. Rogers and was told not to open it until the time was right. It had been several years since Joshua saw Mr. Rogers and never knew what happened to him. Joshua stared at the snow-covered ground where the box was buried near the large oak tree and contemplated if he should dig it up. Joshua decided he would wait until Mary was with him so they could retrieve it together.

Joshua continued to visit other places where he and Mary had memories together. Among the places visited was the park where he proposed, and the spot where the outdoor library center was held. Eventually, he ended up at Tonka State Park where the large tree limb had fallen. Joshua perched himself up on the tree and closed his eyes. He felt the cold air brush across his already frozen face. He took a deep breath and cleared his mind of all the negativity in his life. He relished on how peaceful he felt and how quiet it was until he heard a twig snap. Joshua opened his eyes to see a young man walking by the creek.

"Hello?" Joshua shouted.

The young man stood at the edge of the creek. "This is my tree," he said.

"Well, I guess we are going to have to share it because I'm sitting up here now," Joshua responded.

The young man scoffed.

"Why don't you come up here and we can both sit up here."

"This is my tree. I come here every day and have already claimed this tree, so you best be moving on," the young man replied. Joshua stared at the young man and decided he needed to go.

"Okay, she's all yours." Joshua hopped down the tree as the young man walked over and took his spot.

"That's what I thought," the young man laughed.

"Look, I was done with it anyways. You enjoy your time up there. It's a great place for thinking," Joshua said.

"Whatever," the young man scoffed again.

Joshua walked off taking a few more looks at the young man. He was a little concerned and hoped he was okay but also thought to himself he had enough problems of his own.

Joshua came home to find Mary working on her book. She still wasn't feeling all that well but wanted to work more on her book because she was almost finished.

"Well, hey, you. Where have you been today?" Mary asked.

"It has been a very relaxing day today," Joshua said as he placed his jacket on the chair.

"You doing okay?" Joshua asked as he kissed Mary's forehead.

"I'm actually doing better. I worked on my photo-blogging and my book today and got quite a bit done. This cough, however, is annoying, and I'm super hungry; but other than that, I can't complain."

Joshua kneeled down beside the bed. "How about we order some Chinese-ski?"

"Aw, I miss Benjamin and Michelle. Maybe we can visit them sometime soon."

"That actually sounds like an excellent idea."

"Now, the Chinese food—you are speaking my language," Mary replied as Joshua gazed into Mary's eyes.

"You know you are breathtaking? And, I can't help but to just stare at you. You are the one person that is always there to comfort me. You, you're the best thing to ever happen to me, and I love you for that."

Mary leaned down from the bed to also look into Joshua's eyes. "And you, my sweet husband, are the best thing that has happened to me. I am very blessed to have you in my life. And I love you very much." Mary's stomach growled.

"I'll order us some Chinese," Joshua laughed.

While Joshua was looking for the phone number for the local Chinese restaurant, he told Mary about his adventure and visits he had during the day. He mentioned about the box that Mr. Rogers had given them and asked her if she thought it would be time to dig it up and she agreed. They decided when the snow melted, they would retrieve the box. He also proceeded to tell her of his encounter with a young man at the creek.

"So I was at the spot where the large tree fell across the river when this young guy showed up and demanded that I should leave because it was his tree."

"Oh? Well, what did you do?"

"I decided it wasn't worth arguing over, and I already had my peaceful time there, so I let him have it."

"Well, that was sweet of you, honey. I'm proud of you."

"Yeah. I know. I'm a nice guy," Joshua said as he lay next to his wife. Mary immediately closed the computer.

"I can't read what you are writing?"

"You will soon enough. I'm almost done!" Mary said excitedly.

"Well, I am very proud of you," Joshua said.

"Aw, well, thanks, honey."

Mary started to cough. "Are you sure you're okay? Do you want some cough medicine?" Joshua asked.

"I'm fine. I think I'll go see the doctor tomorrow to see if they can prescribe me something."

"I don't like it when you are sick. I want my Mary to be healthy and happy."

"Well, I may not be healthy right now, but I sure am happy," Mary responded.

"Well, if you are happy, then I am happy," Joshua replied as they both laughed.

The Chinese food was eventually delivered. Joshua and Mary loved their Chinese-food nights. Whenever they had it delivered, they would share moments together and talk for hours. That evening, they talked about life and what their future plans were. After several hours together, Mary decided it was time for bed while Joshua stayed up for another hour as he had something planned for Mary the following day.

The next morning, Mary woke up and didn't feel well at all. She did, however, woke up to find a little sticky note next to her pillow which said, "Good morning, sunshine." She found several other sticky notes as she made her way to the kitchen where Joshua was making breakfast for them both. Mary trudged into the kitchen wearing her robe with a Kleenex in hand. Joshua didn't hear her until she sneezed.

Joshua turned around to see his frail-looking wife. "Aw. Well, good morning, honey."

"Hi," Mary said in a weak tone.

"Is my honey up for breakfast?"

"Actually, I am. Because those eggs look delicious," Mary said.

Joshua continued to prepare the meal. He loved breakfast mornings with his wife. It was a relaxing moment for them both.

"Well, great, because I made them especially for you," Joshua said as he kissed his wife.

"Thank you for the sweet, beautiful notes," Mary said as she kissed him back.

"You're welcome, babe. I just wanted to make today a special day for you because of all you've done for me." Joshua placed the plate of waffles and eggs in front of Mary as she bundled up in her robe. Blankets smelled the food, headed into the kitchen, and waited patiently to lick the plates when they were finished.

"With that said, I do have a day planned for us, if you are up to it," Joshua finished in a singsong voice.

Mary was tired of being cooped up in the house, and although she wasn't feeling well, she was ready to get out. She was also ready to spend a quality day with her husband. After breakfast, the two dressed up warmly and headed over to Charlie's to start their day with a morning-coffee break.

Upon their arrival, they found Charlie had already decorated for the holiday season. Christmas lights were strung around the lampposts that surrounded the outside benches. With the snow beginning to fall fast, it looked like a beautiful winter painting.

Joshua and Mary entered Charlie's Coffee Shop and ordered their drinks. Greg fixed their drinks extra special, topped with a mound of whipped cream. Mary looked around and reminisced about the times she worked there and thought about the day she met Joshua. Apart from the day she was married, meeting Joshua that day was one of the best days of her life. Taking their drinks outside, Joshua and Mary found a spot at one of the benches to sit and talk.

"Do you remember the day we met?" Mary asked.

"I do. You recommended the strawberry frosted with sprinkles," Joshua said as he stared into Mary's eyes.

Mary laughed. "And you said you wanted a dozen of my donuts strawberry sprinkled with frosted."

Joshua chuckled and took a deep breath as he continued gazing into his wife's eyes. "You took my breath away that day. I never knew I would find someone like you, and I wasn't even looking; but there you were, more beautiful than ever. You were so pretty. You are pretty."

The snow continued to fall as Mary and Joshua continued their romantic morning.

"You're my best friend," Mary said.

"You're my best friend too," Joshua responded.

"I heard you guys were here."

"Hey, Charlie!" Mary stood up to give Charlie a hug.

"Hey, boss." Joshua shook Charlie's hand.

"You working today?"

Charlie knew Joshua was off.

"Not today! Spending time with my wife."

"I'm playing with you."

Mary hadn't seen Charlie in a long time.

"How are you doing Mary?"

"I'm doing well. A little under the weather today, but I'm hanging in there."

"Well, good deal. Well, hey, I'll leave you two lovebirds alone. I just wanted to say hello. You take it easy, Mary; and Joshua, you hang on to this one."

Charlie departed as Joshua and Mary finished their conversation and coffee. Mary watched Joshua as he sipped his coffee. "Honey, I want to take a picture of you holding your coffee for my blog."

Joshua was at first reluctant in having his picture on a blog, but he saw how much it meant to Mary, so he agreed. Mary took the photo and then kissed the camera right before she let out a big sneeze.

"Bless you, babe," Joshua said as he moved over to sit by his wife. He rubbed her shoulders and kissed her head. Mary leaned into his body.

"Oh babe, I don't know if I can make it today. Would you take a rain check for another day if we just went home?" Mary asked. Joshua could tell Mary wasn't feeling good and agreed to take her home so she could rest. When they got home, Joshua wrapped Mary up in bed to keep her warm. He kissed her head and her neck. He even smelled her.

"What are you doing, silly?"

"I just love the way you smell, sick and all," Joshua said as he moved Mary's hair out of her eyes.

"Do you want me to stay with you?" Joshua asked.

"I'm okay. I think I'm going to try to get some sleep."

"Okay. I may run to the store or get out so you can sleep. Do you want me to pick you up something?"

"Hmm, surprise me," Mary said as she started to close her eyes. "And be careful, it's starting to get slick out there."

"Okay, I'll surprise you, and I'll be careful." Joshua ran his fingers through Mary's blond hair as she let out a content sigh.

"I love you," Joshua whispered as he kissed Mary's forehead.

"I love you too," Mary said as she started to drift off to sleep.

Blankets came to lay on the bed as Joshua headed out to let his wife rest. Before Joshua headed to the store, he decided to head back to the tree to collect his thoughts again. Upon arriving at the tree, he saw the young man again, sitting where he usually sits.

"Hey, there!" Joshua yelled. "Mind if I sit up there with you?"

The young man looked down at Joshua before blurting out, "Find your own tree, old man."

Joshua continued to walk up the tree and headed toward the young man. "Old man? I'm not that old," Joshua stated as he struggled to get up the snowy tree.

"What do you want, dude?"

"Nothing. I just come up here to think. How about you?" Joshua said as he plopped himself down a few feet from the young man.

"Well, I guess we have something in common because I do the same thing."

"Cool. Cool. My name's Joshua." Joshua held out his hand toward the young man.

The young man had waited for a moment before he reached out his hand. "Matthew," he said.

"So what brings you out here?" Joshua asked.

"What do you care, man?"

"Just trying to make conversation."

Matthew shook his head. "Whatever, dude."

"You know, I come out here to think. Seems like there is always something going on in my life, and I just need time to get away." Joshua said trying to get Matthew to respond.

"Yeah. You ain't kidding. My parents just want to argue, so I come out here to get away from everything," Matthew began to open up.

"So, what's your story?" Matthew continued.

Joshua decided he would just let it all out to the complete stranger.

"Well, I'm married to the most beautiful woman. We can't have children. I found out I was adopted, and I lost my sister when I was about your age." Joshua said as he peeled back a piece of bark from the tree.

Matthew looked up at Joshua. "You lost your sister?" he asked.

"I did."

"What was her name?"

"Amari. Her name was Amari."

Matthew, too, started to peel back the bark from the tree.

"I lost my sister too," he said.

Joshua looked at Matthew. "I'm so sorry, man. What was her name?"

Matthew waited for a minute before responding, "Jessica."

Joshua thought for a moment.

"Did you say, Jessica? Did you, by chance, fill out a prayer card at Heaven's Water Church?"

"Yeah, what about it?"

"You've got to be kidding me." Joshua couldn't believe Matthew was the young boy he had been looking for.

Joshua proceeded to tell Matthew he had been searching him for several months. They talked for several hours about life and loss. As they continued talking, Joshua was amazed at how, out of all the places and all the people he came across, this young boy was the one who he had been trying to find.

Meanwhile, at home, Mary was trying to rest, but her cough was keeping her up. While she was up, she decided to post the picture of Joshua sipping his coffee on her blog. She made a simple comment under the photo which read, "Joshua 1:9." As she finished writing on her blog, she started to cough uncontrollably. She couldn't take it any longer and decided to call the doctor's office to see if they could squeeze her in. With an availability open, she immediately started getting ready. As she struggled to get dressed, she attempted to reach Joshua, but his phone went straight to his voicemail. Within minutes, Mary was out the door to see if she could get some type of relief for her cough.

The doctor's office was packed with coughing children and worn out mom and dad faces. After waiting thirty minutes, the nurse called Mary back. As much as she could, Mary tried to hold back her chronic cough while the nurse was checking her vitals. After the vitals were checked, ten minutes later, the doctor came in.

"Well, how are we today, Mary?"

Dr. Redford had been Mary's doctor for over fifteen years. She was dark-complected and had thick brown hair which reached right past her ears, but it could still be put up in a high pony.

The doctor's white coat fit her perfectly along with her glasses that were black around the edges on the top of the frame. She was one of the best and had the finest communication styles that Mary appreciated.

"Hi, Dr. Redford. I cannot seem to control this cough, and my stomach has been bothering me for about a week."

"Well, let's see if we can get you all fixed up. How are your eating habits?"

"Not too bad. I've kinda been eating junk food more often when I can stomach it."

Dr. Redford looked over Mary's chart.

"How long have you had your cough?"

"I would say about a week or so," Mary said as she coughed into her elbow.

"Poor thing. That is a nasty cough. I think we can get you something for that."

Dr. Redford started typing information on her computer.

"When was your last period, Mary?"

Mary sat there with a dumbfounded look on her face.

"I… I don't remember, to be honest," she replied.

"Has it been over thirty days, do you think?"

"It has been a long time, but I really can't be sure. I used to keep a monthly track of my periods."

"I know you have, sweetie. Well, let's stop gabbing and get you a pregnancy test started, shall we?"

"What—Really? I—is it possible?"

"Oh honey, anything is possible." Dr. Redford left the room to get a pregnancy test.

Mary sat there besides herself. She didn't know what to think, let alone what to say.

"Here you go, sweetie. You can use the room across the hall. Just let me know when you are done."

Dr. Redford left the room as Mary looked down at the pregnancy test in her hands. She closed her eyes and softly prayed to herself.

After her moment with God, she looked frantically for her phone in her purse to call Joshua.

"Voicemail again, ugh." She took a deep breath. "Okay, I can do this."

Mary walked across the hall into the bathroom to begin her test. After several minutes later, Dr. Redford knocked on the door.

"Mary. Honey, are you okay?" There was no answer on the other end. Dr. Redford opened up the door to find Mary in tears, holding the pregnancy test in her hands. Dr. Redford looked down at the test to read the results.

"Well, looks like you might be having a baby." Mary jumped up and hugged Dr. Redford. Dr. Redford was a little shocked by the sporadic hug, but in turn, embraced Mary.

"I've got to find Joshua," Mary said as she wiped her tears away.

"Okay, sweetie. Let's first get a blood test done. We will have final results in a few days."

Mary waited impatiently as her blood work was being done. She tried again to call Joshua with no luck. Her blood pressure was rising, but Mary didn't care. Cold chills ran up and down her skin as she felt God's presence surround her body. She was the happiest she had been in a very long time.

After the blood work, she wrapped things up at the doctor's office and headed straight home in case Joshua was there.

As Mary was on her way home, Joshua was wrapping up his conversation with Matthew. As they said their goodbyes, Joshua looked down at his phone and realized it was off.

Upon arriving at his snow-covered vehicle, he realized he didn't have a charger to charge his phone. He cleaned off the snow and ice off his windshield and drove to the local store to pick up a charger along with some crayons, coloring book, chicken noodle soup, and flowers for Mary.

The snow continued to fall as Mary and Joshua were both headed home to give each other news of what happened to them that day. Joshua's phone finally started to boot up as he was stopped at the stoplight. Mary pulled up to the stoplight and tried to reach Joshua once again. It started ringing.

"Honey, are you there?" Mary asked.

"Yes. Yes, honey, I am here."

"I have something to tell you," they both said to each other.

"Honey," Joshua said on the other line.

"Wait. Wait a minute, honey. Hang on," Mary replied.

"What? Honey, what are you doing?"

Mary stopped her car and opened her door to see a little girl walking into the street to retrieve a ball. There was a truck headed toward her. Mary dropped her phone and attempted to run toward the little girl, however, the snow and the ice on the road made it difficult. The driver saw Mary and the girl and slammed on his truck brakes, sliding on the thick ice. The stopped cars at the intersection looked up to see what was going on, including Joshua.

Mary slid on the ice, reached the little girl, picked her up, and held on tight when the impact occurred. Joshua opened up his car door, darted his way through traffic, and ran as best as he could toward the accident scene, slipping and sliding on the ice. Joshua slowly peered over the truck to see his Mary, appearing lifeless holding a child.

"Mary!" Joshua screamed, falling down next to his wife. "Call 911!" he yelled.

"I'm so sorry. They came out of nowhere," the truck driver stated.

Joshua held his wife and unraveled the little girl from Mary's arms unharmed. She rolled out of Mary's hands and ran toward her parents.

Mary's eyes opened to see Joshua looking down at her.

"Hi, baby," she whispered.

"Baby, what—why," Mary started to close her eyes.

Joshua held on to Mary and stroked her hair trying to get her to speak.

"Baby, stay with me. Stay with me, baby." Mary opened her eyes once again. She looked up at Joshua and smiled.

"I'm pregnant." Mary breathed as she held out her hand to reveal the pregnancy test. Joshua looked down at the test and was silent.

"Baby, it's okay. You're… you're going to be okay, baby," Joshua tried to get Mary to save her strength. He reached behind her head to hold her up when he immediately noticed his hand covered with blood. Mary, slowly drifting away, lifted up her hand to touch Joshua's face.

"I schlove you, Joshua Allen Carpenter."

"I schlove you, Mary Grace Carpenter. Help… help is coming, baby. Hang on. Oh, God, please, baby. Hang on." Joshua's eyes filled with tears.

A tear rolled down Mary's cheek as Joshua brushed her face, wiping away her tear with his hands. Mary reached up and also caught a tear from Joshua's face. She gave a half smile as she stared into her husband's eyes.

"Her name… is Elsie. Our baby's name… is Elsie."

Joshua closed his eyes as tears flooded his face.

"Baby, my book. My book needs an ending. Promise me," she whispered.

"You're going to be fine, baby. Don't… don't talk like that."

"Prom—" Mary started to cough.

"I promise. I promise, baby."

Mary lay there looking up at the clouds. "I see a shell," she said.

Joshua, with tear-filled eyes, smiled and stroked Mary's hair, comforting her. Her eyes were transfixed toward the sky.

He looked up as tears dripped off his chin. His cross necklace dangled around his neck. "I see it too, sweethear—" Joshua looked down to see Mary motionless.

"Mary?"

"Mary? Mary? No, no, no, no, no, no. What… What's happening?"

Joshua started hyperventilating. He searched for a pulse, breath—anything. There was nothing.

He laid his head on her chest and wept uncontrollably, holding her in his arms. Traffic stopped as the sirens roared in the distance. The crowd around him didn't know what to do.

He held on tight to his Mary as he gritted his teeth and cried out to God.

"*Why*! Oh, God, why? You've taken *everything* from me!"

Joshua clenched his fists and gave an evil look up to the heavens as tears rolled down his face when he felt a hand touch his shoulder. He looked up to see an old familiar face wearing glasses with no lenses, staring down at him.

"Mr. Rogers?" Joshua whispered in a stifled tone.

Looking beyond Mr. Rogers, Joshua noticed a little girl across the street holding a basket of seashells. A large truck passed by, and the little girl disappeared in an instant. Joshua continued to look around but could not see where the little girl went. Mr. Rogers knelt down to comfort Joshua. He placed his old hands on Joshua's wet face and brushed away several tears from his cheek.

"Mr. Rogers, what… what are you doing here?"

Joshua held Mary tighter as the paramedics arrived at the scene. Mr. Rogers lifted Joshua's weary head, looked him in the eye, and said just a few simple words, "We have work to do, son."

To be continued.

ABOUT THE AUTHOR

John Hufft has written and illustrated several children's books and is now writing a novel series of faith-based books focusing on life, loss, and love. *The Brokenhearted Christian* is the first book of the series. John writes to inspire others to have faith and keep moving forward when life seems hopeless because we were all born with a God-given purpose. You can connect with John at thechristianbookseries.com.

CPSIA information can be obtained
at www.ICGtesting.com
Printed in the USA
LVHW092151221219
641421LV00001B/56/P